MISSING
IN
PARADISE

Published by Rebelight Publishing Inc.

Rebelight Publishing Inc.
23-845 Dakota St., Suite 314
Winnipeg, Manitoba, Canada
R2M 5M3

www.rebelight.com

Design by Melanie Matheson of Blue Claw Studio, Winnipeg, MB

Issued in print and electronic formats
ISBN 978-0-9939390-2-0 (pbk)
ISBN 978-0-9939390-3-7 (epub)

Printed and bound in Canada
10 9 8 7 6 5 4 3 2 1

MISSING IN PARADISE

A NOVEL

LARRY VERSTRAETE

2014 rebel!ght PUBLISHING INC.

For Jo

CHAPTER 1

A BUNCH OF THINGS SURPRISED ME on the morning of Gram's garage sale.

#1: Stinking weather.

Dad dragged me out of bed at sunrise on the hottest, muggiest day of my entire fourteen years. The sheets were glued to my chest, and my pyjama bottoms stuck like extra skin in places they normally wouldn't. Sweat squished in my shoes as I walked to the car, and it dribbled down my neck, plastering hair to the back of my head. Yeah. That miserable.

 # 2: Cruddy drop-off.

Dad dropped us off at the curb in front of Gram's rambling old house. "Take care of your little sister, Nate," he said. "Give your grandmother a hand. Stay out of trouble. Think you can manage that for three days while your mother and I are away?"

I stared at the front door. The last time I visited was right after Gramps' funeral. I didn't want to be here. Not with Gramps gone. Not with Gram so weepy. And definitely not at this ungodly hour.

Gram ran down the steps to greet us, followed by Buster, Gramps' old golden retriever. Mom hugged Olivia, then me and Gram. She patted Buster and scrambled back into the car. Just like that my parents were off, squealing tires down the street as if they couldn't wait to escape.

#3: Mountains of stuff.

When I stepped into the house, my mouth dropped open. I'm no neat freak, but seeing Gramps' stuff piled up everywhere—mind-boggling! In the four months since his death, Gram had given away heaps of Gramps' stuff, dishing it out like Santa Claus to relatives and neighbours. The garage sale marked the final step of her purge, a last-ditch effort to get rid of rusty saws, battered skis, moth-eaten clothes and a billion other useless things.

"Sell everything, Nate. *Ev-ery-thing*. I want it all gone." Those were Gram's words.

I felt like saying, yeah, like that's going to happen. But I didn't. Who's going to come to a garage sale on such a crappy day for junk like this? On a scale of one to ten, I gave the chance of success a big, fat zero.

#4: Junk that sold.

Okay, I was wrong. Hordes of people came. Most arrived way too early. Don't they have lives? In less than an hour, the mountains of crap dissolved into small hills. People will buy almost anything if the price is right.

And that's pretty much when #5 on my list happened. I didn't realize it at the time, but it unleashed an entirely new batch of surprises.

As I straightened a heap of shoes, Buster scrambled to his feet in a frenzy of yips and yelps. A split second later, a blast of cold air ripped through the garage. An icy hand seemed to clamp down on my shoulder and squeeze. Goose bumps the size of golf balls ran up my arm. I shivered uncontrollably. My teeth even chattered.

I looked around. Three tables over, Gram chatted with a customer. Beside her, Olivia clutched a naked Barbie with chewed off toes. Simon, my friend from next door, stood by the *Books for Sale* table with his nose in a comic. While I shivered, everybody else plowed through Gramps' stuff as if nothing happened.

So weird.

A second later, the icy feeling vanished. Heat and humidity shot up again. Buster circled the table beside me and pawed at something below. Then he sat on his haunches and howled pitifully, the saddest song you've ever heard.

"What's the matter, old boy?" I asked.

Buster pawed the floor a few more times and then lay down. I stooped to pat his head, but he just stayed there, sprawled out like a doggie doormat on the concrete. He stared straight ahead, pressing his nose against a cardboard box tucked underneath the table.

The box, covered in layers of masking tape, looked ordinary, sturdy and about the size of a small microwave oven. A label, scrawled in black marker, ran across the top and sides: *Garden Supplies*. There was no mistaking the handwriting. Crisp, sharp letters sloped forwards. Both *p*'s widely looped. Gramps' writing, for sure.

"Come on, Buster. Move, will ya?"

But he didn't.

I tugged his collar and patted him again. "Come on. Let's see what you've found."

As Buster struggled to his feet, his gaze didn't leave the box. And when I hoisted it up on the table, he sat like a prison guard, watching.

I grabbed a knife from the tool display, sliced the tape and opened the flaps. Inside, a neatly folded drab blue shirt covered something else. I pulled out the shirt. Several buttons were missing. The collar was frayed and dark seams ran down sleeves that were bleached almost white. Next, I pulled out a brown leather briefcase with two handles. Tiny scratches etched the worn surface, and a deep gash ran across the front flap like a scar along a prize-fighter's arm. Curious, I fidgeted with the tarnished clasp to open it. Pinprick stabs rippled between my shoulder blades. Goose bumps returned. My fingers froze. I felt eyes tunnelling right through me.

Someone was watching.

A dark figure stood in the sunlit doorway. I couldn't make out the exact features, but I knew it was old man Fortier, Gram's neighbour. His gimp leg gave him away, throwing him off balance, forcing him to lean on his cane. It couldn't be anyone else.

Gramps never trusted Fortier—a mutual feeling, I figured. A running feud between the two of them started when Fortier moved next door five years ago. Something about a dispute over a property line. Gramps called Fortier "the criminal next door." Once, I'd heard Fortier mutter "damn cheat" behind Gramps' back.

Fortier moved out of the bright sunlight and stepped closer. He looked from the briefcase to the shirt, back to the briefcase, and then to the box. He tilted his head to one side as if reading the label. He limped closer. "Where'd you find this?" Fortier ran a hand across his whiskery face and wiped off a bit of slobber that had pooled around his lips. He leaned on his cane and reached out to touch the briefcase.

I yanked the case away and almost knocked Fortier over. I turned my back to him and stuffed the briefcase and shirt into the box. Finally Fortier, the creep, took the hint. He hobbled away, muttering under his breath.

It took a while for the goose bumps to disappear. There was something unearthly about the whole episode, something totally freakish about the sudden wind, Buster's behaviour, and the way the box appeared out of nowhere. I couldn't shake the feeling that Gramps had somehow staged the entire show just for me, that somehow he reached beyond the grave to bring the box to my attention. Now that I found it, I had to keep it out of Fortier's hands. I was sure of that. I just wasn't sure why.

CHAPTER 2

I hid the box under heaps of clothes and checked throughout the day to make sure it was still there. I looked for other boxes like it too, but I had a hunch I'd found the only one.

Fortier hovered over Gram, fussing with price tags, folding clothes and pretending to be useful. But whenever Gram veered away to help customers, he poked into piles and searched under tables. Twice I switched the location of the box when Fortier came too near. Finally, I stashed it inside a cabinet beside Gramps' workbench.

"Buster. Here boy," I called. "Sit."

I patted Buster, pointed to Fortier and whispered, "Watch him, okay? Let me know if he gets close."

Buster flopped on the floor, eyes glued to Fortier.

"Good boy."

I helped an old lady haul a ratty armchair to her car, then organized a sagging pile of worn magazines. As I carried a floor lamp past Simon, he waved a comic book in my face. "Nate. See this? Batman. First edition. Can you believe it?"

Simon looked like a lost orphan child. Tuffs of hair stuck out like propeller blades around his head. A smear of jam ringed his mouth. His three-sizes-too-big t-shirt flapped like a tent around his skinny chest.

Simon's mother moved to England to start her life over when he was just a toddler. She never called, never even sent Simon a card on his birthday, so it's like he didn't have a mother. His grandparents lived in different cities, and for years, babysitters drifted through the house. When Simon turned twelve, the situation changed. After that, his father, away on business and working long hours, pretty much let Simon run free.

Sometimes I envied Simon with no annoying sister or demanding parents and the house to himself. Simon could do whatever he wanted without anyone nagging him. But other times I felt sorry for him, alone so often.

"Batman. First edition. That's great, Simon." I plopped the lamp on the floor beside a pair of old stereo speakers and glanced around. Where was Fortier now?

"You want to come over later?" Simon asked.

"Maybe. I have a few things to do first."

Two tables away, Fortier rifled through the jewelry display with a gaudy necklace clenched in his fist.

"We could play video games," Simon said hopefully.

"Uh huh."

"Or we could watch TV."

"I suppose."

"Or we could just hang out."

A flash of movement caught my eye. Fortier thumped away from the jewelry display and toward us.

Simon's eyes widened. "Farter!" His nickname for Fortier. Even funnier because Fortier's first name was "Albert." A. Farter. Hilarious!

But Simon wasn't laughing. Faster than you could say "Batman," he scooted to the kitchen appliances on the other side of the garage.

I couldn't blame him for hiding. A few months ago, Fortier caught Simon rummaging through the lumber pile at the side of his garage. He grabbed Simon by the shoulders and screamed at him. In spite of a stroke years ago, Fortier was still a strong man. He scared Simon silly. Since then Simon steered clear of Fortier, his house, his yard—everything.

I held my breath. Fortier drifted closer to the workbench. Once again, I felt the overwhelming urge to protect the box, to keep it safe from him.

By four o'clock, the garage sale ended, drawing to a close the hottest, stickiest, longest day ever. Simon left early. He wobbled home, his pencil-thin arms loaded with broken electronics that Gram happily let him have. Buster stayed at his post. Fortier, the two-faced sleaze, hung around to the end, shuffling after Gram and pretending to be her knight in shining armour.

I swept the floor, then packed left-over picture frames into a crate, all the while looking for an opportunity to investigate the box on my own.

"Do you have room for one more?"

Gram's voice broke my concentration. She stood beside me holding a faded black-and-white photograph in an ornate picture frame. "I don't know what I was thinking. These things shouldn't have gone into the garage sale. I'm so glad they didn't sell."

I looked over my shoulder. Fortier? Fortunately, the old goat was crouched under a table on the other side of the garage.

"Sorry, Gram. What did you say?"

Her eyes misted as she drew me to the window. Light spilled across the photograph. Four figures stared out of it, dressed in clothes that might have been snatched from a dumpster.

"Do you know who these people are, Nate?"

"That's you, isn't it?" I pointed to a girl in the picture who looked about five years old.

"That's right. And this is my mother. Your great-grandmother. That's my brother and...," Gram drew a deep breath. "And this—"

Buster woofed frantically, drowning out whatever else Gram said. I wheeled around to see a storm of tiny ball bearings ping like metallic rain across the concrete floor. Fortier stood at the workbench, shaking his head and cursing. "Crazy mutt. Look what he made me do. Practically gave me a heart attack."

Buster glanced at me. Some people say dogs can't smile, but I swear Buster wore a grin so wide you could have hung a coat on it.

Olivia ran over to help. Fortier rounded up bearings with his cane while she made a game of scooping them into the box.

"Glad at least one of these kids respects their elders," Fortier muttered.

Whatever, Fortier.

I turned back to Gram's photograph. "Go on, Gram." I pointed to the fourth figure in the picture—a short, slim unsmiling man with wavy black hair. "Who's this? Your father?"

Gram stashed the picture in the box and took her time answering. "Every family has its share of secrets, Nate. My father, Tom Hendricks, is ours. I was too young to remember much about him, but my mother told me he was a scoundrel. He abandoned us, left us high and dry at a time when we needed him most." She picked up an old sweater of Gramps' and cradled it in her arm. "So many memories here. Sorry, Nate. It's been a difficult day."

"I know, Gram." I really didn't know what else to say.

CHAPTER 3

Fortunately, Fortier hobbled home soon after the ball bearings were picked up. Gram hurried into the kitchen to make dinner. Olivia followed, saying she wanted to help. Her stomach growled, and I suspect she was more interested in sampling food than actually making it.

I grabbed the mysterious box and barreled up the creaky stairs to the second storey. Buster crept behind, his nails click-clattering on oak hardwood. I charged past Olivia's room and then Grams', but when I approached the closed door to Gramps' office, I slowed. So did Buster. I shook off a chill and headed left down a wood-paneled hall to a room with a dormer window and low sloped ceilings. Mom's old room, now mine whenever I visited.

I closed the door, set the box on the carpet between the bed and the dresser, and sat beside it. Buster curled his long body around mine as I dug into the box for the faded shirt. No tags identified the size, but I guessed it was a medium. Too small for Gramps, who wore a size larger, like me. A solid red circle covered the back, like a bulls-eye on a pale blue target.

The briefcase was more battered than I first realized. Scuffs covered the faded leather. One of the front pockets was torn. Faint scratches ringed the tarnished clasp that held the flap closed. Two faint letters were engraved on its surface: MP.

Dishes clattered from the kitchen below and Olivia's shrill voice echoed through the floor. "Oh, Gram! That smells delicious."

I had a half-hour or less before dinner.

I pried open the clasp, reached inside the briefcase and pulled out a wad of paper bundled around several small objects: a few buttons, ivory-white and roughly the same size and colour as those on the shirt;

a tin cup, dented, the lip folded back; a carved wooden pipe that reeked
of stale tobacco.

I placed the objects on the floor and leaned back for a better look.
Why label the box *Garden Supplies* when these things had nothing to
do with gardening? And who did this stuff belong to anyway? The
ordinary buttons and tin cup could be anyone's, but the other objects
didn't suit Gramps. The shirt wasn't his size. Gramps never smoked
and wouldn't allow anyone else to smoke in the house, so why would
he own a pipe? The briefcase didn't seem to be his either. The clasp
said MP, not HW for Harold Wheeler.

Digging into the briefcase again, I pulled out a map of Manitoba, its
creases still razor sharp, like new. I opened it and spread it on the floor.
A section of provincial highway had been highlighted in yellow. At the
western edge of the province where the highlighted line ended, a few
handwritten words were etched into the page.

Shipment #35–GOLD.

Gold?

"Nate," Gram called. "Dinner's ready."

The forward scrawl. The firmly crossed *t*. Gramps' handwriting.
What did it mean?

Seconds later, a knock sounded at the door. "Nate, Gram called you
for dinner," Olivia said.

I scrambled to my feet. Buster rose with me. "Yeah, just a sec."

Gramps had written something else on the map. Four more words
near the others. I squinted to bring them into focus.

Mildred must not know.

What didn't Gramps want Gram to know?

"Nate, are you coming?" Olivia banged the door again. "I'm hungry!
Hurry up!"

"Yeah, yeah, Ollie," I sputtered. "I'll be right down."

I tried stepping to the door, but my feet felt like they'd been nailed to
the floor. Buster took one step and stopped too. He whimpered softly
and nudged my hand. He'd felt it too. I know he did.

CHAPTER 4

Slowly, as if someone granted me permission to move again, the nailed-down feeling vanished. I hurtled down the stairs, enticed by a salty aroma. I rounded the corner and froze in the doorway.

Fortier. Sitting in Gramps' spot at the dining room table.

"We're celebrating tonight," Gram explained, catching my stunned look.

Tiny and slightly built, Gram looked a whole lot younger than her age. Though her hair was completely grey, she had smooth skin with few of the sags and bags most old people have. The past few months had dragged her down, but tonight her blue eyes sparkled.

Gram reserved the dining room for special celebrations. Tonight's meal must have ranked as some kind of special, though. Tall candles stood at both ends of the long table. Paper placemats decorated with Chinese symbols were in position, one at each end and at each side. Platters heaped with rice, chow mein, dim sum and other Chinese dishes dotted the table. Soft Oriental music twanged from the CD player in the living room.

"I didn't have time to cook, so I ordered in," Gram said. "I hope you don't mind."

I didn't mind at all. I loved Chinese. But what the devil was Fortier doing here?

Gram seemed to read my mind. "Oh, Nate. I invited Albert to join us. He's been such a dear, dropping around all week, checking up on me and lending a hand. Here, Nate." She guided me to a chair opposite Fortier.

"Hurry," Olivia waved her chopsticks like an orchestra conductor leading a symphony. "I'm hungry."

I faked surprise. "Again?"

Gram passed Olivia a carton of chicken chow mein. "Never mind your brother, Ollie. Come, dig in."

As I settled in, Buster curled into a ball by Olivia's chair, the best place for a free meal. When Olivia dumped half of the carton onto her plate, Buster followed her movements, ready to snatch bits that missed the target.

While Olivia attacked her food, I locked my eyes on Fortier. His blue-grey eyes returned my stare with a steady gaze. He nodded curtly and seemed to force a half-smile. Fortier had cleaned himself up. Gone were the morning's whiskers on his long, boney face. From across the table, I caught the sweet scent of after-shave mingling with the sharper smells of soya sauce and ginger. He'd put on a fresh white shirt—no stains yet on this one—and gunked up his hair with some kind of goop so it stayed plastered in place.

"Wait," Gram said. She raised her glass of water in a toast. "Here's to a job well done. To a most successful garage sale."

I clinked glasses with Olivia and then Gram, but when Fortier raised his glass in my direction, I ignored him and took a long guzzle of water.

Gram wasn't finished. "Here's to you, Nate. You too, Olivia. Thank you for all your help. Also to you, Albert. You've been such a dear friend."

I sputtered and gagged.

Dinner passed slowly. Olivia wielded her chopsticks like nunchuks, too busy for more than a few words. Gram and Fortier blubbered to each other, passing comments and compliments in equal measure.

I kept quiet and looked for distractions. My eye caught the framed photographs along one wall. Some photos were black-and-white, others color, but all pictured family members past and present. Lots were of Gramps. Gramps with his two daughters. Gramps in a business suit, ready for work. Gramps and Gram at their forty-fifth wedding anniversary. Gramps, everywhere.

I swallowed a lump in my throat. Although Olivia looked like a McCormick—Dad's side of the family—I looked more like Mom's side, especially Gramps. For the first time, I saw my resemblance to him in the photos of his early years. We shared the same broad shoulders, same square jaw, same hazel eyes. We even had the same patch of stubborn brown hair that stuck up at the back like a flag flapping in the breeze.

Despite the heat, I shivered. Like before, goose bumps crawled up my arms. The strange nailed-down feeling I'd had upstairs was still fresh. Gramps, reaching out wanting…something.

An explosion of laughter brought me back to the table. Gram tee-tered on the edge of her chair, clutching the sides of the table. Tears streamed from her eyes. Fortier smiled broadly, as if he was pretty pleased with himself. What did he say that was so funny?

I fumed, for the first time more angry at Gram than at Fortier. How dare she invite him for dinner, with Gramps barely dead four months? Especially knowing how Gramps felt about Fortier.

When Fortier suffered a stroke four years ago, Gramps seemed to think justice had been finally served. "God's revenge," he called it at the time. What did Fortier think when he heard the news that Gramps had been found dead in his car? Was justice served then?

"Oh, my!" Gram said. "I forgot the most important thing."

She slipped from the room. I chased noodles across my plate, stick-handling them to one side to avoid Fortier's gaze. When I finally looked up, I found Fortier equally occupied. He had taken out a pen and was doodling on his placemat.

Fortier cleared his throat. "So Nate, your grandmother says that you were a big help today."

I fought a particularly stubborn noodle and concentrated on steering it past clumps of sticky rice. "Hmph," I said, not giving Fortier the satisfaction of a real answer.

Fortier tried again. "You seemed to be busy the whole time."

"Hmph." More stick-handling.

He shoots….

The noodle slid through puddles of soya sauce to join its compan-ions on the far side of the plate.

Fortier cleared his throat. "So did you find anything interesting?"

I dropped the chopsticks and grabbed the table to steady myself. Fortier stared at me, his yellow teeth showing through a thin smile.

Gram returned with a bowl of fortune cookies. "Here we are. I don't know how I forgot these." She handed the bowl to Fortier. He plucked one out, apparently forgetting the question he'd just asked me.

As Gram and Fortier compared fortunes and Olivia licked her plate clean, my grip on the table relaxed. I puzzled over the strangely marked box and the stuff inside. The map with the highlighted highway route. The messages written on it.

Shipment #35 – GOLD.

Mildred must not know.

What did Gram say earlier? Every family has its share of secrets. How many secrets did our family have?

CHAPTER 5

Time crawled by. Fortier rattled on about some fishing trip he had planned for the next day. Gram listened with rapt attention. Olivia, meanwhile, stuffed her face. God, the kid could eat! All in all, it was pretty disgusting.

Fortunately the phone rang, giving me an excuse to escape. I bolted to the kitchen, almost dumping my glass of water as I fled the table. I caught the phone on the third ring.

"Wha-took-ya so long?" Simon said. I could barely hear him over the monotonous music and the rat-tat-tat of gunfire blaring from a video game.

"Never mind," I said. "What's up?"

"Coming over?"

"Yeah, sure." I wanted to scream yes, but I tried not to sound desperate. "Soon as I can."

"Drawbridge. Fifteen minutes?"

"Right."

Coming back from the kitchen, I found Fortier standing beside Gram. She laughed hysterically. "Albert, that is so funny."

I choked back a groan and detoured around the table to avoid Fortier. As I passed his chair, I caught sight of his placemat. Squiggles lined the edges. In one corner, Fortier had drawn a crude box. He'd written something on its side, but I couldn't make out what it said.

I grabbed two fortune cookies and muttered, "Going over to Simon's."

Gram waved cheerily, hardly even glancing up. Buster scrambled from his place at Olivia's feet, tail swishing like a high speed wiper blade.

"Sorry, fella." I patted his head and edged away. "Not this time."

"Wait for me, Nate."

Olivia. The last thing I wanted was my little sister tagging along. "You can't come, Ollie."

"But why?" Her eyes swelled into watery oceans. A tear rolled down her cheek. She sniffled.

Crap. I forced gentleness into my voice. "Ollie, wouldn't you rather stay with Gram? She'll need your help, and you wouldn't want to miss ice cream would you?"

"But Nate…." She ran her tongue over her lips and looked to the kitchen. Dessert was her favorite part of any meal. "Okay, next time."

"Sure thing."

I bolted out the door, down the sloping back yard, and crept through weeds to a stand of trees along the winding river below Gram's house.

Simon was already there, holding a plastic bag and standing at the end of a board that crossed a dip in the ground at the base of the tallest tree. He waved cheerily at first, then dropped his hand and stood at attention.

I stepped on the creaky board.

"Ah, aren't you forgetting something?" Simon said.

"I am?"

"You know."

"Oh, yeah." I rolled my eyes, but kept a straight face and bowed. "Permission to cross over, Me Lord?"

Simon bowed in return. "Permission granted, Nate McCormick, Knight of the Realm."

Simon Sloan and I had been friends as far back as I could remember. He was two years younger than me, but the age difference never mattered much. Every time I visited, we hung around together. Lately, the visits had become less frequent. I'd been away at camp the past couple of summers, for one thing. And when Gramps became sick…well, I just couldn't.

The tree behind Simon—a giant maple with wide spreading branches—towered above all the others. Our tree. Simon's and mine. Three summers ago, we lugged boards from his place, rigged a pulley to one of the maple's branches, and hauled the lumber up two storeys to build a tree house. We hammered together a floor in a wide crotch of the tree, attached walls and a roof, added a ladder, and furnished it with cast-offs from Gramps' junk collection.

Afterwards, on each visit to my grandparents', we reinforced the wobbly structure and added new features. We kept our hideaway a secret, carefully erasing our tracks and telling no one of its whereabouts.

Well, almost no one. Simon's father knew and, of course, I had to tell Gram and Gramps where I was spending so much time. They didn't mind. Just be careful, they told me. Don't fall. Stay out of the river.

"You been here lately?" I asked.

"Nope. Not since that last time."

I expected as much. We had an unspoken agreement. The tree house was joint property. Neither one of us entered it without the other.

Holding the bag in one hand, Simon took the lead up the ladder. When his foot hit the third rung, the wood creaked. Nails popped. He hesitated.

"Come on, Simon. Make up your mind. You going up?"

"Easy for you," he yelled back. "You're not the one risking your life."

He scrambled up the last four rungs. I followed, wary of each creak and pop. When I reached the trap door at the top, Simon offered his hand. I laughed.

"You really think that's going to work?"

I outweighed Simon. One yank from me and he'd be on the ground, faster than a speeding bullet.

The interior of the tree house was a mess. Piles of acorn shells littered the floor, and the cushions that once served as our chairs were gnawed and shredded. Squirrels. The place smelled of decay, a musty combination of rotting leaves and putrid squirrel droppings.

Disgusting.

We swept the floor and scraped away gobs of squirrel poop, tossing the clumps out of the trap door. I found a hammer inside a rusty toolbox and pounded in a few nails to stabilize the structure. Simon spread an old blanket on the floor. We flopped on it, side-by-side, carefully avoiding wet or dark spots. Stretched out like that, my legs hit the opposite wall, and Simon's shoulders brushed mine. The last time I'd been there, we had plenty of room. Now it felt cramped and tight.

"Here." I passed a fortune cookie to Simon.

Simon opened his bag and hauled out sandwiches, a bag of chips, three apples and a chocolate bar.

"Help yourself," he said.

"Thanks. I just had dinner."

"Yeah? So did I."

Neither of us spoke for a time. I chugged a soda while Simon munched on a thickly layered peanut butter and jelly sandwich.

Simon pulled a plastic block from his pocket. "Want to play?"

I stared at the antique device. "Is that a Game Boy?" So many scratches etched the plastic that it looked like it had been tossed in a blender.

"Yep. Beautiful isn't it? Found it broken in someone's trash, but I fixed it."

"How'd you manage that?"

Simon launched into a long description of disconnected wires and new solder. I zoned out and thought of Fortier. He was up to something, I could feel it. An image of the box popped into my head. The map. *Shipment #35 – GOLD. Mildred must not know.*

What was that all about anyway?

Suddenly, I noticed Simon's silence.

"Remember the last time we were here?" he said finally. Bits of sandwich shot from his overstuffed mouth. It's a wonder he didn't gag.

"You were scared silly."

"I was scared? You were the one bawling and screaming."

When we had finished the tree house, we figured a sleepover was in order. Simon begged his father for permission. Since I was staying with my grandparents that weekend, I hounded them for the same. Finally, after some intense nagging, they agreed.

On a moonless night, so pitch black that we couldn't see anything without Simon's flashlight, we settled into our sleeping bags. The wind picked up, rocking the tree and swaying the tree house. Branches scraped the roof, filling the night with spooky sounds.

"You were so scared," Simon repeated. He broke into a fit of giggles. "I thought you'd wet your sleeping bag."

"You were just as scared," I shot back. "Neither of us lasted long. Remember?"

Simon squelched a final giggle. "Yeah. I guess that's the best part. The storm. Oooh, oooh."

Around midnight, the storm broke. Lightning flashed. Thunder boomed loud and near, rattling the tree. We freaked and abandoned our sleeping bags. Scrambled down the ladder in inky blackness.

Ran like scared rabbits—right into two ghostly figures by a tent at the bottom of the tree. Gramps and Mr. Sloan. Seems they had secretly set up camp to watch over us.

"I'm not sure who was more surprised—them or us," I said.

"Us. Definitely us!"

We laughed and then lapsed into a long silence.

"You miss him?"

The sudden seriousness of Simon's voice startled me. I knew exactly who he meant. I shrugged. "Yeah. I do."

"Me too." Simon voice was so soft I could barely make out the words.

That surprised me. I'd never thought of it like that before—that Simon would miss Gramps too. But they'd been neighbours and in many ways Gramps had been as close to Simon as he had been to me—like he'd been Simon's grandfather too.

'I saw him…you know, the day he died," Simon said slowly.

I swallowed a wave of guilt. That morning, Gramps had called to invite me over. He sounded excited. Something about going somewhere, about wanting me along. I blubbered an excuse. Not today. Maybe another time. I just couldn't go. Not with Gramps losing more of his brain every day to Alzheimer's. Not with him acting weird and so different than the Gramps I knew.

"You saw him? Where?"

"By the garage. Putting something into the car trunk. A shovel, I think. I remember being surprised because your grandmother wasn't there. It wasn't like her not to be with him…you know…because of his, um…."

"Condition?"

"Yeah. Condition. Your grandmother watched him like a hawk. But that morning, he smiled and joked like his old self. I thought your grandmother knew he was out there. Honest I did."

"What did he say?"

"Not much. He wondered how school was going, how my dad was doing, normal stuff like that." Simon drew a long breath. "Really, he made perfect sense, Nate. Right up to the end."

"The end?"

"When I asked where he was going, he laughed. 'Got some loose ends to tie up, Simon. There's a shipment coming in.' That's all. Then he got in the car and drove off. I never gave it another thought until I found out he was missing."

The hair on my neck stood on end. "You sure that's what he said, 'a shipment's coming in?'"

"Positive." Simon scrunched up his face. "What does that mean?"

I ignored his question. Although I counted Simon as my best friend, it didn't feel right to say more. If it didn't make sense to me, how could I possibly explain it to him?

We sat for a while, side-by-side, gazing at the spread of trees before us. We hadn't really talked about Gramps after the funeral, not until now.

Simon finally broke the silence. "Want to play?"

For the next hour we took turns playing video games. But my heart wasn't in it. I kept seeing the map with the yellow line leading northwest, straight to the words Gramps scrawled there.

Shipment #35 – GOLD.

CHAPTER 6

On the way back to Gram's, I stopped by the garage in her backyard. Gramps' old brown Buick stood in front of it, dust-covered from months of sitting idle. After Gramps' death, Gram refused to drive the car. She said she just couldn't. Even though she lived on a meager pension, she bought another car right away. Still, she hung on to the old one. Strange considering how quickly she rid herself of Gramps' other things.

I stared at the Buick, took a deep breath, and reached for the door handle. Gramps died in that car. Did I really want to do this? I fought an urge to bolt, but finally open the door and slid behind the steering wheel to the spot where Gramps once sat. A trickle of sweat dribbled down my back. Despite the steamy heat, I shivered.

What might it have been like? Did Gramps know he was about to die? Was he disappointed I wasn't along? What was he thinking in those final moments, far from home, far from family and friends with his mind broken?

I never cried at the funeral and not since either. I wouldn't let myself. Not with Gram, my mother and Aunt Carol crying enough tears to take a raft down. Not with men like Uncle Phil and my father dry-eyed and holding back their grief. But now I cried. Blubbering gushes rolled down my cheeks. I sobbed and clenched the steering wheel until my knuckles turned white.

For a long time, I sat in the car, not wanting to stop, not being able to. Then, as if a mysterious force suddenly turned off the taps, the tears ended. I wiped my face with my t-shirt, exhausted yet strangely relieved.

In the growing darkness, I ran my hand across the upholstery and along the dash, searched the glove compartment and under the seats, but found nothing. I popped the trunk and clamored out of the car into the sticky night air. Inside the trunk, I discovered a tattered blanket, a plastic garbage bag, and—just as Simon said when he described Gramps' last morning—a shovel. Otherwise the trunk was clean. No trace of dirt, no clumps of loose soil.

I breezed into the house through the back door. Gram stood at the kitchen sink humming softly as she filled the tea pot with boiling water. Dirty dishes sat in crooked piles on the counter.

"Olivia is asleep," Gram pointed to the bedrooms above. "But we were just about to have tea. Care to join us?"

We? "Fortier's still here?"

"Albert's in the living room. Why don't you go sit with him until the tea is ready?"

Either Gram didn't hear the disgust in my voice or she chose to ignore it. "Me? I...but ... ." A voice inside me screamed at Gram. Have you lost your mind? The guy was Gramps' worst enemy. Now he's your friend? Get real.

Somehow I managed to hush the inner voice. It wasn't easy.

While Gram took cups out of the china cabinet, I edged to the sink, opened the door below, found the trash can and fished through gummy rice, sticky noodles and soggy coffee grounds.

"Oh my. That will never do," Gram said, just as my hand curled around a moist sheet of paper.

"What will never do?" I dug out the paper, pried off a damp noodle and stole a peek at it. Fortier's placemat, soggy, but still intact. I stuffed it into my back pocket.

"This cup is chipped. It was one of my favourites too." Gram tsked a few times. "I'll have to find another. Tell Albert I'll be there in a minute, will you?"

I slipped into the living room, but Fortier was nowhere in sight. I breathed easier. Maybe the guy had slithered home. I could only hope.

Head down, I bolted up the stairs. Halfway up, I bumped into Fortier. He fumbled with his cane, steering his feet in different directions as if he couldn't decide whether to head up the stairs or down. From his stunned expression, I knew he hadn't expected to meet me along the way.

"Just looking for the bathroom," he said.

"There's one on the main floor." I pointed to the hallway beside the living room.

"Thank you, Nate," Fortier said, polite as can be. He turned awkwardly, thumped down the steps with his cane and limped around the corner. "Thanks again," he said before joining Gram in the living room.

All that sweetness. What a joke. I tore up the stairs. At the top, I stopped. The door to Gramps' office was closed. I barreled past, turned left down a wood-paneled hall and stopped.

The door to my room was open.

CHAPTER 7

I flicked on the light to find Buster curled in a furry heap on the floor. I ran to the closet and flung open the doors. The box and other things were still there—right where I left them.

What was Buster doing here? Had Fortier been in the room? I thought I'd closed the door on my way to dinner, but had I? I tried to recall my movements. Leaving the room, grabbing the door handle—

"Nate, come join us." Gram called.

I itched to examine the items again. "There's a shipment coming in," Gramps told Simon before driving off in his car. Had he been heading to the place on the map? To the spot where he'd marked *Shipment #35 – GOLD*?

With Buster trailing behind, I left the room to join Gram and Fortier, to fake politeness, smile, nod my head, agree even when I disagreed, and do absolutely nothing to arouse suspicion or let Fortier know I was on to him.

Gram had no idea what kind of man she was dealing with. But I did. Fortier was after something. I knew it even if Gram didn't.

Fortier stayed longer than expected. Fortunately, Gram noticed my bored look and stifled yawns. "Why, Nate, I'm sorry. You must be exhausted after such a long day, and here I am keeping you up."

I said goodnight as sweetly as I could—not easy. Buster followed, apparently just as bored as me. Upstairs I examined each object in the box. The shirt, buttons, tin cup, pipe—nothing linked them to Gramps or to something called Shipment #35. There was nothing more inside the briefcase, either. Except....

I uncrumpled the wad of paper containing several small objects. It was an advertising flyer, a handout promoting coming events.

✦ Giant Sale ✦ and Auction

the flyer announced in bold letters. Below, in smaller print, faint and weathered words read:

Collectibles, Antiques, Memorabilia, Rare Items
You'll find them all at Paradise's annual sale and auction
August 12-15
Everyone Welcome!

I searched the map again, located Shipment #35, and noted the towns and villages in the area. Just south of Shipment #35, I found a dot, barely a pinprick on the map, and beside it the name of a town.

Paradise.

I read the flyer again. A small bit of print at the bottom caught my eye.

PARADISE—A PRAIRIE GARDEN OF EDEN.

Oh, Gramps. Either you were being very clever or you were very confused. Which was it?

CHAPTER 8

Sometime after midnight, I pitched myself into bed but I couldn't sleep. My mind reeled with questions. Gramps had travelled to Paradise at some point; the flyer proved it. Although I didn't know for sure, I suspected the objects in the box came from there too.

Paradise—A Prairie Garden of Eden, the flyer said. Gramps had labeled the box *Garden Supplies*. Coincidence? Or had Gramps purposely chosen a title to remind him of its contents, but keep it hidden from everyone else? Maybe. But it was just as possible that Gramps had simply been confused. Putting the wrong name on a box fit the profile of someone with Alzheimer's disease, someone slowly losing his mind.

Down below, dishes clinked between bursts of laughter. Fortier, chumming up to Gram. My fingers curled into a fist. My stomach churned. I tried sleeping again. Useless. Finally, I abandoned the idea and crept out of the room leaving Buster whimpering softly in his sleep. I tiptoed down the dark hall to Gramps' office.

Musty, stale air greeted me the moment I stepped inside. Everything looked as I remembered it. Gramps' massive roll top desk along the far wall. Shelves crammed with books beside it. By the window, Gramps' binoculars. No footprints on the carpet. An even layer of dust on the furniture. No one had entered the room in a long time, not even to fetch things for the garage sale.

In five or six steps, I stood at Gramps' desk, his belongings spread before me. Reading glasses folded and ready to use. Sketchbook, open to the first page. A stack of papers neatly arranged. A row of pencils by their side. Running my hand along Gramps' leather chair, I lingered for a moment over the well-worn place where he once rested his head. Had it really been four months? It felt like yesterday.

I conducted a thorough search of the room, starting with the book-case and then moving to the bills, receipts and letters stacked on the desk. All were dead ends—not a single mention of Shipment #35 and not a hint of lost gold.

Next, I tackled Gramps' sketchbook. After retiring, Gramps took up drawing. He carried a coil-bound sketchbook everywhere and spent hours at his new hobby. Most of the sketches were line drawings of the neighbourhood. The winding river. Tulips in Mr. Latimer's garden. An old shed on the Phillips property two doors down.

As I flipped through the sketchbook, I noticed changes in Gramps' style. The further I got into the pages, the more haphazard the draw-ings appeared. Familiar objects looked distorted, out of proportion, and larger or smaller than in real life with thick, bold lines and dark, gloomy shades.

Was it the Alzheimer's? The last few sketches looked especially weird. One showed a gnarled stump beside a creek, another a rectan-gular stone protruding from the ground, and a third, a half-buried log protruding from the mud. A small date scrawled at the bottom of each sketch said August 12.

August 12? One of the dates on the Paradise flyer.

I pulled out desk drawers and reached into compartments. Most of the contents appeared ordinary—file folders, pencils, paper clips, art supplies. Deep inside one drawer, below a heavy notepad, my fin-gers curled around something soft and rectangular. I tugged it from the drawer—a brown vinyl folder containing two photographs and a typed letter.

One of the photographs—a faded black-and-white picture—showed a dozen sturdy buildings, each built of thick, vertical wooden planks and roughly the size of a two-car garage. The buildings stood in a forest clearing, but nothing identified their location or purpose. The second photo—also black-and-white—showed an aerial view of a lake surrounded by trees. Buildings dotted a nearby meadow. A road tunnelled through the thick forest beyond it.

I unfolded the letter, typed on official Bank of Montreal stationery.

Dear Mr. Wheeler,

In response to your query about Shipment #35, which disappeared some-where north of the Paradise region of Manitoba, please be informed that the gold coins have never been recovered. Despite numerous investigations into the matter over a course of decades, the whereabouts of Shipment #35 is still unknown.

*   The Bank of Montreal has a vested interest in recapturing its holdings, however, and would welcome any additional information you might be able to provide about the missing shipment. You might be interested in knowing that a reward exists for its recovery. Because of the increased value of gold over the years, this amount is a substantial one.*

I sank into the chair and re-read the letter. Missing gold. Reward. So Shipment #35 was real after all. Finding the shipment would be like winning the lottery. Dollar signs danced in my head, conjuring images of super-sized TVs, a sports car when I turned sixteen, season tickets to NHL games for Simon and me, endless chocolate sundaes for Olivia, and maybe even a trip to Mexico for Gram and my parents.

Maybe Gramps hadn't been so confused after all. I checked the date at the top of the letter—written over two years ago, long before Alzheimer's claimed a sizeable portion of Gramps' brain. I read the letter again and flipped it over to check the back. A familiar scrawl snaked along the top of the page. Gramps' handwriting. Four words, same as before.

Mildred must not know.

Suddenly, the room felt stifling hot, the air thicker and heavier than ever. I heard footsteps creak across the floor downstairs, and Fortier's gruff voice.

"Good night, Mildred. I'll drop by tomorrow before I leave."

Gram softly replied, "Thanks for all your help today, Albert." And then the screen door squeaked open.

I moved to the window and watched Fortier limp home, his cane thumping the concrete driveway. I grabbed the binoculars and focused on the old man as he approached his garage. Fortier fumbled with the door handle, pulled the garage door up, flicked on the light and hobbled inside. I spotted a stack of boxes inside the garage. The top one looked familiar. Size of a small microwave oven. Layers of masking tape around it. I caught a small glimpse of the black marker scrawled on the side. *Garde…*

I blinked. My hand trembled. Too soon the door closed.

CHAPTER 9

I waited for Gram to go bed before leaving Gramps' office. Then I crept down the hall, weaving past creaky boards that might wake her. When I entered my room, Buster lavished me with long wet licks.

"Good boy." I patted Buster and gave him a hug. Too tired for more, I collapsed on the bed and fell asleep in an instant. The busy day must have stirred up something inside me, though. I dreamed. Many times. All through the night. Dreams so vivid they seemed real.

Dream #1.
Fortier creeps up the stairs. He wears a silly smile on his long face and uses his cane as a guide. Reaching the top, he stops at a closed door. He grabs the handle. A cold breeze shoots out from underneath. Fortier fumbles, teeters for a second then crashes to the floor, a heap of thrashing arms and legs. He spews cuss words, some new to me.

I woke up then. Fortier's cusses echoed in my head. Despite its creepiness, the dream entertained me. I replayed it a dozen more times before falling asleep again.

Dream #2. Also Dreams #3, 4, 5, 6....
I run through brilliant light, my feet flying over a hard, uneven surface I can't identify. The light blinds me. I can't tell where I am. I'm almost out of breath, nearly exhausted. Now and again, I glance over my shoulder as if expecting to see something there, but there never is. Then, as I round a curve, I feel a clammy presence, a light touch on my shoulder, a hand pressing down, someone leaning on me, trying to get close and—

That's when I woke up every time, dripping with sweat, my heart racing, the sheets clenched in my hands. For a few minutes, I'd just lie there, forcing calm into my mind. After a while, I'd fall asleep again, but each time the dream returned. Same uneven surface. Same bright light. Same eerie sensation. Waking up to sweaty sheets and panic.

CHAPTER 10

When the phone next to my bed rang, hazy light streamed through the curtains. The house was quiet, Olivia and Gram likely still asleep. Fighting the soggy sheets, I grabbed the receiver.

"Nate, that you?" Simon asked.

I glanced at the clock. "It's only six. What's so urgent?"

"Coming over?"

I hadn't slept much. Not with eerie dreams repeating. Not with my string of questions.

"Nate? You still there?"

"Yeah," I mumbled. "I'll be over later." After hanging up, I slipped into a dreamless sleep that seemed to last only a minute. Then the phone rang again. I planted one foot on the floor, arm poised to rip the phone off the hook, but then the ringing stopped.

From downstairs, I heard Gram's voice and Olivia's giggle. The smell of freshly brewed coffee wafted into the room. I glanced at the clock. Eight? What, already?

I stumbled down the hall to the bathroom, threw water on my face, ran a comb through my hair and tried to tame the stubborn patch on top. When I returned to my room, I scooped all the items back into Gramps' box, stashed it on the upper shelf in the closet, closed the door and crept down the stairs with Buster leading the way.

"Oh, Nate. Simon called a few minutes ago." Gram sounded cheery.

"Yeah." I said. 'I'm not surprised."

Olivia sat at the kitchen table, slurping soggy Cheerios. Beside the bowl stood naked Barbie propped up on her half-chewed feet and a new addition to Olivia's collection—G.I. Joe, dressed in camouflage fatigues so filthy they looked like they'd been dipped in mud. Olivia positioned the two so they faced each other, Barbie's lips locked in a plastic smile, Joe's eyes glaring back in his I-mean-business way.

For a fleeting second, I wondered how many hands had touched the grimy pair, how many germs they carried, and whether Olivia would be on the national news soon: *Winnipeg Kid Spreads Killer Doll Virus.*

"I found a friend for Barbie," Olivia said between mouthfuls.

"I can see that."

Buster settled at the base of Olivia's chair. He watched each transfer of the spoon, ready to scoop up Cheerios before they hit the floor.

"You must be starving." Gram placed a large plate of eggs, ham and toast in front of me. "Come. Eat something."

In minutes, I gulped down the entire offering, barely stopping to chew. I washed it all down with a giant glass of orange juice.

"Got to go," I said, scrambling for the door.

Gram grabbed my arm and steered me back to the table. "Sit down for a few minutes, Nate. It's been so busy we really haven't had a chance to talk." Gram pulled her chair closer to mine. She started to say something, but stopped. She studied me long and hard. Her eyes grew watery. She sighed. Her hand reached up to pat my unruly thatch of hair then dropped to her side.

I squirmed. Right then, I knew that Gram wasn't really looking at me. It was Gramps she was seeing in me instead. "Ah, Simon's waiting for me. I really should go."

Gram's distant look vanished. "Sorry, Nate. It's just that—"

"Can I watch TV, Gram?" Olivia wiggled off her chair, Barbie in one hand, Joe in the other. Stray Cheerios plastered her cheeks.

"Why sure, sweetheart." Gram peeled bits of cereal off Olivia and gave her a hug before sending her off. "Where were we, Nate?" she asked.

"I'm not sure."

A hundred discussion points raced through my head. Gramps. Shipment #35. *Mildred must not know.* "Gram, what happened to Gramps on his last day?"

Gram's shoulders sagged. The lines around her mouth tightened. Her hand fell heavily to her side.

Instantly, I regretted the question. With my parents, the subject of Gramps' last day was taboo. No one wanted to talk about it.

"Someday, I'll tell you," my mother had said, brushing the question aside when I asked her about it shortly after the funeral. "It's too soon. I...I just can't." And so I'd never learned the exact details—just that Gramps' death had been sudden and the circumstances unusual.

"Never mind. Let's talk about something else," I said.

"No, Nate. You deserve to know what happened and I need to talk about it as well."

Gram grabbed a napkin and dabbed her eyes. "When your grandfather was first diagnosed with Alzheimer's, we hardly noticed the signs. He had trouble remembering things like names and faces, or where he left his keys. But in his case, the condition worsened quickly. Everything about him changed in a matter of months."

Gram twisted the napkin and began tearing it into bits. "He had his good days, of course. That last morning was one of his better ones. I thought that as long as he stayed in his office, he would be okay. So I did laundry in the basement. I didn't hear him leave. It wasn't until I called him for lunch that I realized he was missing."

Sound blasted from the living room. Through the doorway, I saw Olivia standing in a trance in front of the TV with Barbie and Joe in choke holds, as the Count from Sesame Street ran through his numbers. "A one...a two...a three...."

"Ollie, dear," Gram called. "Could you turn that down just a little?"

I smiled. Gram did too. Getting Olivia's attention now was a lost cause.

The napkin lay on the table in shreds. Gram reached for another and dabbed her eyes again. "Where was I? Oh, yes. A passing motorist found your grandfather in his car on the side of a road near Minnedosa. He was already dead. It probably happened quickly. A massive heart attack, the doctor said. I doubt he felt anything."

An image flickered into mind. Gramps' map. I remembered another dot just below Paradise, not far away along the same highway. The town of Minnedosa.

"Why would Gramps go there?"

Gram brushed away another tear. "I don't know. No one does."

She lapsed into a long silence. "First my father. Then Harold," she said so quietly I could barely hear. "Twice in one lifetime. No one should have to endure that."

I played with napkin bits and stared at the table, not sure what to say. Buster wandered over. He wore a crown of soggy Cheerios. A drizzle of milk ran down his snout.

"Missed some, boy." I laughed.

Gram laughed too. While I plucked gummy Cheerios off Buster, Gram wiped his muzzle with a napkin. "There. All cleaned up." Gram ran her hand along Buster's long coat and looked into the dog's eyes. "Buster really came through for your grandfather, you know."

"He did?"

"Buster was in the car with him. The police told me the dog wouldn't leave, not even when paramedics arrived."

I studied my hands and swallowed hard. Gramps' phone call. His invitation. I should have been there, not Buster.

As if reading my mind, Gram put her hand over mine. "The past is the past, Nate. There's nothing we can do to change it." She sighed, brushing crumbs and napkin shreds off the table. "We don't get second chances in life for some things. Make the best of each day, I say. Now you'd better get over to Simon's before he calls again." She winked and smiled. "That boy isn't the most patient person, is he?"

I had one foot out the door when Gram called me back. "I've asked Albert to help me clean windows before he leaves. Think you could give us a hand?"

I tore through the overgrown hedge that separated Gram's house from Simon's with one thought in my head: Fortier, you weasel. Just what are you after?

CHAPTER II

The Sloan house, easily the oldest and largest on the block, was covered in stone and built like a giant layer cake, three floors piled high. Grass as tall as my knees covered most of the backyard, while at the front, weeds choked the life out of struggling flowers. In six years, Mr. Sloan had done little to improve or maintain the place. Apparently his standards weren't at all like my dad's, who woke me up at dawn three times a week, insisting I mow the grass and pluck every weed.

I raced up the stairs to Simon's room on the third storey, through a ramshackle collection of wandering hallways and tacky rooms that had been painted and wallpapered dozens of times. The Tower. That's what Simon called it. Smaller than the other two storeys and off-center from the rest of the house, the third floor looked like a medieval tower. At least according to Simon, who had a wild imagination.

Cast-offs filled the room, probably rescued from trash bins or dragged home from neighbourhood garage sales. I steered around Simon's unmade bed, past a small refrigerator buried under a heap of clothes and a microwave oven perched on a rickety TV table.

Simon stood with his back to me at a long, cluttered table in the "sanctuary"—his name for a far-off corner by the window where he kept his most precious stuff. The table held bottles; bundles of paper; an ancient computer, printer and phone; a half-eaten sandwich; and a giant geranium plant—the product of one of Simon's more successful science experiments a few years ago.

"Sorry I took so long," I said. "What's so urgent?"

Simon turned around.

I stopped dead. My mouth hung open. I almost swallowed my tongue.

Simon smiled and shrugged.

My eyes travelled from Simon's blackened face to his ink-stained hands, and then up again to the smudges that ringed his eyes. "What are you doing?" I sputtered.

"I got tired of waiting," Simon said. "I started without you."

"Started what exactly? You look like a racoon on a bad day."

Simon stepped to the side and ran his hand over a clunky photo-copier in the center of the table behind him. "Beauty, isn't it? Found it in a dumpster outside Staples. Wasn't working, but I got it going. See?"

He pointed to a bulletin board above the table, proud as a new father looking at his first child. The bulletin board sagged under the weight of newspaper clippings, maps, photographs and dead center, stapled ran-domly like birdshot, a cluster of smudged black-and-white photocopies.

"Those two are the best," Simon tapped a grainy reproduction of a chunk of Lego and an even grainier photocopy of his Game Boy. "I'd gotten the hang of it by then."

He swung around, oozing excitement. "Want to try it?"

We spent the next fifteen minutes photocopying everything in the room from leaves off the geranium plant to Simon's Spiderman under-wear. We plastered the bulletin board with our collection, then stood back to admire it like two artists gazing at their masterpieces.

"Awesome." Simon turned to give me a high five.

I high fived him back. "Yeah. Awesome."

For a few minutes, we stood side-by-side, soaking up the wonder of our work.

"You know," Simon said at last. "Maybe we should try something different."

"Like what?"

Simon glanced at me. His eyebrows shot up. A smile crept across his lips. "I think we should photocopy our butts."

I stepped back. "You can't be serious."

"Come on. It'll be fun."

"No way."

"Just think. They're like fingerprints. No two the same."

"No!"

"Suit yourself," Simon pushed a chair to the table. "You don't know what fun you'll be missing." He climbed the chair, dropped his pants, slid down his underwear and planted his bare bottom on the scanner. "Ooo...nice and warm." He pointed to the start button at the base of the machine. "Lend a hand, will ya? Fire away when ready!"

I groaned, but pressed the button anyway. The photocopier clattered and whirred, and finally spit out a copy.

Simon hopped down, his pants and underwear around his ankles. He craned his neck for a look. "Well, whad-ya think?"

A peach-shaped object stared at us. "Too dark," I said. "Let's try another."

Simon adjusted a few buttons, climbed up again and wiggled into position. "Smile for the camera," he giggled.

A much clearer copy emerged from the machine – Simon's tiny butt in all its detailed glory. "Beauty," Simon said, holding it at arm's length.

"Sure is."

"Your turn," Simon pushed me to the chair.

"Ah...."

"Don't be such a chicken."

"I don't think—"

"Come on. Live a little, will ya!"

"Well...um...okay. But just one copy. There's no way I'm doing this twice."

Simon manned the photocopier, laughing the whole time. I climbed the chair, dropped my drawers, and slid into position on the glass flat-bed. "Pretty toasty up here. Blast away, Simon!"

As it was, we spent thirty minutes photocopying our butts, adjusting contrast, trying different angles, applying different pressures, all in our quest for perfect copies. We stopped when the scanner grew so hot it almost seared our bottoms. By then a mountain of paper had grown on the floor, butts and more butts, Simon's and mine mixed together.

"Getting hard to tell whose is whose," I said as I picked through the pile.

Simon plucked one off the floor and shoved it in my face. "This one's yours. It's bigger and see that dimple? It's like your signature."

We each chose our best one. Simon cleared a space on the bulletin board and stapled them up. Then he whipped out his cell phone, held it up above his head and aimed it at the butt pictures behind us. "Move in. We gotta get a shot of this."

I groaned, but smiled for the picture anyway. "You're not going to post this or show it around, are you?"

Simon didn't answer, just snapped another one. "You gonna take one too?" he asked.

"Nope. We've got more than enough, don't you think?"

He handed me the cell phone and pulled a couple of sodas from the fridge. "Awesome picture, isn't it?"

"Yeah, great. A selfie of two buttheads and two butts."

"A two butt-head selfie!" Simon roared.

We collapsed on the bed, rolling in laughter. "A two-butt-er!" Simon squealed. "You kill me, Nate!" He ripped open a bag of chips and flipped on his TV to a grainy re-run of the Simpsons we'd seen a half-dozen times—a classic episode with Bart, Homer and Lisa up to their usual stuff. "Wait for it," he said. "This is when Bart says to Homer...."

During a commercial break, we foraged through Simon's little refrigerator. We found a few chocolate puddings as well as more sodas.

"You sure you have to go home tomorrow?" Simon's voice sounded heavy, a notch deeper than usual.

" 'Fraid so." I punched Simon softly on his shoulder.

He punched me back. We watched a few commercials and swished our puddings in silence.

With so much time gone helping Gram yesterday, I hadn't seen Simon all that much. The kid had some dumb ideas. He knew how to sucker me in too. But sitting in his room now reminded me of how much fun Simon was and how I'd missed him. If only we could spend more time together.

I was about to say something when the Simpsons came back on to show Homer phoning Moe, the bartender. We edged closer to the TV screen, halfway into laughter already. A classic moment was coming, one of the show's famous crank calls.

"Hello. I'd like to speak with a Mr. Snotball," Homer said to Moe. "First name Eura."

Simon slapped the bed and snorted loudly. "Eura Snotball?" he said at the exact moment Moe did.

We laughed and spilled soda on the bed when Moe finally figured things out.

"What? How dare you! If I find out who this is, I'll staple a flag to your butt and mail you to Iran!"

"Want to try that out?" I said.

"Mail your butt to Iran? Sure, I've got a copy—right over there." Simon pointed at the bulletin board.

I slugged him with a pillow. "Not that, Butt Boy. Want to make some crank calls?"

Simon practically danced off the bed, twitching in nervous excitement. "Oh yeah, let's." He grabbed his phone. I took out mine.

For the next hour, we tested some classic Simpson lines on friends and relatives, disguising our voices.

"Is there an Ivanna Tinkle there?" I asked Randy Sturgis, a friend from school. Unfortunately, Randy recognized my voice right way, which took most of the fun out of the game.

Simon called his cousin, Trevor. "I'm looking for Amanda Huggenkiss."

Trevor was a natural born sucker if ever there was one. "Amanda Huggenkiss?" he repeated three times before catching on.

We made a half dozen other calls, using Simpson favourites like "Is there a Butz there? Seymour Butz?" and "Do you have a Bea O'Problem at home?"

I laughed so hard my sides ached. My arm burned from all of the punches Simon delivered. Then I had an idea.

"Let's call Fortier."

Simon stopped in mid-giggle. "Farter? You sure?"

"Yeah. Come on," I said. "It'll be fun."

Simon gulped and flashed a weak smile. "Well, okay."

We found Fortier's number online and I dialed. Part of me wished he had already left for Gram's. The other part hoped for a chance to pull a fast one on the old man. The phone rang four times before a raspy voice answered. Fortier for sure.

I lowered my voice and disguised it with a southern twang. I put the phone into speaker mode so Simon could hear too. "Is there a Mike Rotch there?"

Fortier fell into the trap. "Mike Rotch? There's no Mike Rotch here."

Simon giggled and spurt a mouthful of soda across the room. I coughed trying to stifle a laugh.

"Who is this?" Fortier growled. "Is this your idea of fun? Harassing an old man?"

I froze.

"Hang up," Simon whispered. "Nate, hang up."

I did, but not before Fortier said one last thing.

"Nate, is that you?"

CHAPTER 12

I left Simon's around eleven o'clock after promising to see him later. Clouds hid the sun, but the sopping humidity stayed. I slipped through the hedge, my t-shirt dripping with sweat. I couldn't wait to trade my heavy jeans for a pair of shorts.

Two voices carried across the yard, one deep and gravelly, another soft and lilting: Fortier and Gram. Crap. I'd forgotten the old man was coming over.

Gram waved a towel and called hello. Fortier muttered something from his wobbly perch on a stepladder below the kitchen window. Without looking up, he dipped a sponge into a bucket of water and slopped it along the window sill.

Olivia ran over with Barbie and G.I. Joe in one hand, and in the other, a Transformer missing an arm and a leg.

"Look what I found. Isn't he pretty?" she chirped.

"Here, Nate." Gram handed me the towel. "Why don't you take over while I slip inside and get lunch started? Ollie, would you give me a hand?"

"I'm really not hungry," I said.

Actually, I felt sick. Chocolate pudding, potato chips, soda, eggs and ham churned in my stomach like toxic stew. I squelched a burning burp and swallowed to keep it all down.

With Gram and Olivia gone, Fortier attacked the window, wiping faster and harder than before. The ladder rocked and teetered. I fought the bubbling surge in my stomach and watched, weak-kneed, half-hoping Fortier might come crashing down.

Fortier sprayed glass cleaner and wiped the window, then stopped and glared at me. "You know, Nate. Your grandmother thinks the world of you."

Perfect timing, Fortier. I'm about to hurl.

Fortier ignored my pained expression. He looked around and dropped his voice to a whisper. "As for me, I don't know you that well, so the jury's still out. But I do have a bit of advice."

Make it quick, Fortier.

"There are laws about doing what you did." he said. "Harassing someone is a crime, you know."

Fortier sneered and turned back to the window.

What was it Gramps called Fortier? The criminal next door? An image from the previous evening floated into my head. Fortier's garage. Gramps' box. *Garden Supplies.*

"Stealing stuff from your neighbor is a crime too," I said.

Fortier's froze in mid-swipe. "What are you talking about?"

"You know."

I didn't get to say more. I bolted into the house, hand over my mouth, past Gram and Olivia in the kitchen, past Buster sprawled on the floor in the hallway, straight to the bathroom. I arrived not a moment too soon.

God, but I felt sick.

CHAPTER 13

I recovered quickly, but lunch was out of the question.

"I don't think you have a fever," Gram said, putting her hand on my forehead, "but maybe you should rest a while."

I climbed the stairs slowly, feeling better with each step. Buster plodded patiently behind. The door to my room was open. Across the freshly vacuumed carpet, man-sized footprints staggered unevenly around the bed, to the desk and then to the closet.

I tore open the closet door, pushed aside hanging clothes, and found the box. Nothing looked touched, but the encounter confirmed what I suspected. Fortier had one box. Now he wanted the other. He probably knew about the gold too.

As I whipped off my jeans to change into shorts, a wrinkled paper dropped to the floor. Fortier's placemat. I'd completely forgotten about it. I unfolded the paper, pried off a splatter of chow mein, and spread the placemat on the floor. Fortier had drawn a box in the top right corner and below it a series of lines with dots on them, each labelled with a letter of the alphabet. Just below the box, where the longest line ended, Fortier had drawn a fish beside the letter P.

Why a fish? Did it have anything to do with his planned fishing trip?

I examined the jumbled lines again. Inside the box, Fortier had printed a number. Thirty-five. The lines and letters, I'd seen them before. I searched through Gramps' box and found the map of Manitoba. Fortier's drawing matched. The lines were highways leading northwest. The letters stood for towns along the way. M for Minnedosa. P for Paradise.

Fortier, you crafty devil.

Once again I examined each object in the box, hoping to discover something new, but quickly gave up. None of it made any sense.

Buster circled around me and rested his paw on my knee.

"You were with Gramps, weren't you? You know something, don't you? Okay, Buster. Spill the beans."

Buster stared back, ears perked, head cocked to one side. If only dogs could talk. But dogs didn't, and Buster had already done his part. The rest was up to me. But I needed help. Fortunately, I knew just where to get it.

I grabbed the box and fled down the stairs, bypassed the dining room by going out the front door, and raced through the hedge. Thick clouds drifted across the sky, whipped by a steady, warm breeze. Humidity hung in the air like a sopping wet towel. By the time I reached Simon's, my hands were so sweaty I almost dropped the box.

Simon sat at his computer in front of a flickering screen. He wore a bike helmet wired with Christmas lights and a rabbit-ear antenna from an ancient TV. A long electrical cord ran from the helmet to a set of speakers he'd rescued from an old stereo.

"What are you doing?" I peeked at the monitor. A title in neon colours blazed across the screen: *How to Communicate With Aliens*. "You can't be serious."

"Shh…listen. Can you hear that?"

I put my ear right up to the speaker. "Yeah. It's call static. What were you expecting? Martians?"

Simon twisted a joy stick and turned up the volume. "Now?"

"More static. Will you just put that down for a minute? I need your help."

Simon swung his chair around. He pulled off the bike helmet, eyed the box under my arm and craned his head for a better look at the label. "*Garden Supplies?*"

"Not really."

I set the box down, pulled out the shirt and briefcase, and laid everything on the floor. Simon's eyes lit up when I launched into the story about finding the box. They grew wider still when I showed him the map, the location of Shipment #35, and the words *Mildred must not know.*

Simon ran his fingers over the box. "So your grandfather really was going after a shipment. Gold! A fortune in gold!"

When I described Fortier, his interest in the box, his helpfulness to Gram and the way he'd been sneaking through her house, Simon couldn't contain himself. "Farter," he squeaked. "What a snake! What a low-down, dirty, rotten, no-good—"

"Wait, there's more," I said. "Fortier has a box just like this. Same size, same label. I saw it in his garage."

"What a sleaze. How'd he get that?"

"I'm not sure, but here's something else I found." I pulled out the wrinkled placemat and spread it on the bed.

"What is it?"

"You know that Fortier is going on a fishing trip, right?"

"Good riddance."

"Well, take a look at this."

Simon squinted to bring the jumbled lines into focus. "I don't get it. What's it mean?"

I ran my finger down the lines, giving Simon a guided tour. "See here's Winnipeg. There's Minnedosa. That's Paradise. See the box with thirty-five in it? That's the location of the gold."

Simon scratched his head. "Okay. So? I still don't get it."

"The fish. See the fish Fortier drew there?" I stabbed the placemat with my finger. "I don't think Fortier is really going fishing at all. He's going for Gramps' gold."

"Oh." Simon's eyes grew to large glowing orbs. "Oh, I see. Why that low-down, dirty, rotten…." He ranted for a full minute. "…What a sneak, what a bum, what a…."

I let Simon unwind. I knew from experience it was better that way.

Finally, Simon stopped and drew a deep breath. "What are you going to do about it? You're not going to let Farter just steal your grandfather's gold, are you?"

"Umm." I leaned back and scanned the placemat again. "We don't have a lot of evidence. It's just a hunch."

I'm surprised our brains didn't start smoking as they ground through the options and sifted through the possibilities, looking for some way to find proof of Fortier's evil intentions.

In the end, we realized proof was just forty metres away.

CHAPTER 14

As we crept around the corner of Fortier's garage, Simon grabbed my arm and glanced around. "You sure Farter is at your grandmother's?"

"Pretty sure. He's probably still having lunch. I don't think he finished cleaning the windows either."

Simon scanned Gram's driveway. "You're positive?"

While Simon kept lookout by the side of the garage, I lifted the door. I expected it to be locked, but it squealed and squeaked as it rumbled along the rusty track.

"The whole world's gonna hear us," Simon hissed.

I raised the door just enough to shimmy underneath. Then I crawled inside across the clammy concrete. Fortier had left the trunk of his green car open. A two-seater red canoe sat on the floor beside the car, ready to load on to the roof rack. Was Fortier packing for his fishing trip?

Simon peeked under the door. "Well?" he whispered. "Whad-ya find?"

"Give me a minute, will you?"

There was no sign of the box, just an imprint in the dust where it once stood by the door. I scanned the trunk, taking inventory.

"He's packed a sleeping bag, tent, small cooler. He's got a metal toolbox here too, and a shovel. And, oh yeah, an axe."

"No fishing gear?"

"Nope."

Tucked into the dark reaches of the trunk, I spotted an open cardboard box. It looked like a perfect match to the one from the garage sale. Same size. Same masking tape. Same title in Gramps' hand. *Garden Supplies.*

I reached inside, dug around, and felt the cool hardness of something metallic about the size and shape of a hockey puck. I hauled it out.

A distant door slammed. A cane thunked against concrete, followed by a gruff voice. "I'll be right back, Mildred."

"Oh my God," Simon squealed. "Farter's coming!"

I pocketed the object, crawled under the door, and ran. There wasn't time to close the trunk or shut the garage door.

Simon ducked behind trash bins at the side of the garage. I hid behind the front bushes. Even from this distance, I could see Simon's eyes, big as hubcaps.

Fortier limped home. He crossed onto his yard and stopped. "What the...?"

A string of curses followed. Fortier swung around. He looked up and down the street. As his gaze swept the bushes, I sank into the thick branches.

Still cursing, Fortier opened the garage door the rest of the way and flicked on the lights. He searched the trunk, muttering constantly. Finally he slammed the lid, limped outside again, glanced around and shrugged. Then he shut off the lights and pulled down the door.

I waited until the screeching faded before motioning Simon over.

"That was close." Simon sounded like he'd inhaled a jug of helium.

We bolted back to Simon's and threw ourselves on the bed in a fit of laughter.

"So, whad-ya find?" Simon asked, once he regained control.

I hauled the puck-shaped object out of my pocket and rubbed my thumb over the tarnished brass shell. "Looks like an old compass." A hair-thin crack ran across the glass cover, but the needle swung freely. I squinted to read the tiny script engraved on the back. "Northern Airways."

"Northern Airways," Simon echoed.

I hopped off the bed and spread the contents of the box on the floor. What a jumble of disconnected junk. A tattered blue shirt, too small for Gramps, with a red circle logo on the back. A well-worn briefcase with the letters MP engraved on the clasp. Assorted buttons, a dented tin cup, an old pipe. And now a brass compass with Northern Airways etched on the back.

The click-clack of Simon's fingers tripping along the keyboard caught my attention. "Still looking for aliens?" I asked.

"Nope." He waved me over. "You gotta see this."

A website called *Canadian Airlines Past and Present* flickered across the screen. Simon clicked on item #15 and a new page appeared. *Northern Airways*. Black and white photographs of airplanes from long ago materialized—single engine, twin engine, biplanes and others.

"Wow. Neat," Simon said.

I pointed to the fine print along the bottom and read it out loud.

A privately owned company founded in 1934, Northern Airways serviced the northern regions of the Prairie Provinces with a fleet of 8 planes. Due to a series of financial failures, including the disappearance of the company's largest plane and its million dollar shipment of gold coins, Northern Airways declared bankruptcy and went into receivership in the late 1940s.

"Wow. Neat," Simon repeated.

"You know what this means?"

"Yeah. Farter's a dirty, no good, sleazy—"

"Not just that," I held the compass up. "The gold was aboard a plane. We're looking for a wreck or something like it."

Suddenly, the room darkened. We moved to the window and watched storm clouds sweep past. Pellets of rain—a few drops, then a cascade—splattered to the ground. Lightning flashed, brilliant white, followed by a boom of thunder that shook the house.

Simon edged closer to me. "Jeez, get a load of that."

The hair on my arm bristled. A wave of goose bumps appeared. Simon shivered and clenched his teeth. "What the...? What's going on, Nate?"

I knew it wasn't the storm, but Gramps visiting again. Only how could I explain that to Simon without sounding like a complete nutcase?

Once again I kept quiet, convinced more than ever that Gramps wanted me to find the gold and finish the job he couldn't.

CHAPTER 15

The storm persisted, splashing rain against the glass and rocking the house with thunder. Simon turned on the lights and hovered a safe distance from the window, clearly spooked. "Did you feel that?"

I ran my fingers over the compass and examined it again. Fortier was heading to Paradise. Of that I felt certain. What a creep. Using Gram. Pretending to be all concerned about helping her while poking around her house to gather information. All for the gold. Not fair. Not right.

"We have to get there first," I said.

Simon sat on the bed with his feet dangling off the side, tuned into the Simpsons. He wielded the remote like a light sabre. "Get where?"

"Paradise. That's where Fortier's heading. We have to get there before him to find the gold."

"Say what?"

"We've got to figure out some way of getting to Paradise. And we can't tell Gram, either."

Gramps' message: *Mildred must not know.* Why didn't he tell her?

"Okay," Simon said slowly. His feet danced along the floor and his mouth hung open like a toothy cave of questions. "How will we do that?"

We tossed ideas around. Most of Simon's were pretty extreme.

 # 1: Take Gramps' old car.

Sure, like Gram would never notice it missing. Besides, who's going to drive it? Not me.

 # 2: Hitchhike.

Don't those situations end badly? People vanish without a trace, or bodies appear beside the road. No thanks. Next idea.

 # 3: Hop a ride with Fortier.

Okay, like that's going to work. Don't you think he's going to notice two kids in the back seat?

I threw another idea into the mix. "We could take the bus. I bet Greyhound goes to Paradise."

In a flash, we were at the keyboard, but this time my fingers did the work and Simon gave directions. We found Greyhound's website, scanned bus routes, searched schedules and figured out the cost of tickets.

"Yeah, that might work," Simon said, rubbing his hands eagerly.

"How are we going to get away without anyone noticing?" I asked.

We watched lightning flash through the window in rapid-fire bursts, as if somehow that would give us the answer. And in a way, it did. A flood of lightning illuminated the river bottom. One tree stood out from the others, taller than the rest, branches spread wide like welcoming arms.

Our tree. Simon's and mine.

"Sleepovers," we said together.

Our plans mushroomed and quickly took shape.

"Money." I said. "We'll need some for the bus, plus more for supplies."

Simon dragged his Darth Vader bank to the bed and dumped the contents. I tore through my pockets and added a few bills my parents had given me.

"Food?"

Simon opened his refrigerator. "What's your pleasure? There's more in the kitchen downstairs too."

I looked at my watch. "We better hurry. The bus leaves at three and it's already one-fifteen. We haven't even figured out how to get to the bus terminal."

"Relax." Simon said. "You're talking to an expert. How do you think I get around this city?"

We ironed out a few more details then I left, promising to return in half-an-hour.

"A real treasure hunt! This is going to be fun," Simon said gleefully.

I raced from the house. When I neared the hedge, doubts surfaced. What if we got lost? Or caught? Or encountered danger? What if Fortier discovered our plans? Or found the gold before we did? As I pushed through the tangled hedge with rain pelting me and lightning flashing, fun was the last thing on my mind.

CHAPTER 16

Huffing, I flung open the screen door and barreled into the house. Fortier sat at the kitchen table sipping coffee. Gram leaned over the counter, laying slices of chocolate cake on plates.

"Just in time." Gram pointed to the table. "I know how much you like chocolate."

"I...I...I'm not really hungry." It was the truth. Sort of. My stomach churned like a washing machine, not from nausea this time, but from worry.

Seeing Fortier didn't help. He shot me a killing look and gave me the once over, starting with my feet and working up to my head. "Where were you?"

"Simon's. Why?"

Fortier harrumphed. "Of course. Innocent as always."

Gram didn't say a word in my defense which really bugged me, but I swallowed my pride. "Gram, would it be okay if I slept over at Simon's tonight?"

"Tonight?" She turned to face me. "I don't know. Earlier, you said you weren't feeling well."

"I'm fine now. Pleeease. It's my last night here and I probably won't see Simon for a while. Pleeease."

Fortier rolled his eyes.

"I thought you were going fishing," I said to him.

"Waiting for the storm to pass," he muttered, shaking his head.

"Please, Gram," I begged again. "Just for one night."

"Well." Gram stared at the hedge through the window. "You won't be very far away, I suppose."

Fortier grunted. He narrowed his eyes, shooting daggers of doubt my way. "Not far at all. Right, Nate?"

I put my hands in my pockets and shifted uncomfortably. Did Fortier know? How was that possible? "Please, Gram," I said, ignoring him. "Simon is alone a lot. He really could use a friend."

Gram heaved a heavy sigh. "Well alright, as long as it's okay with Simon's father. But you have to be back tomorrow evening before your parents return. And no sleeping in the tree house. Not in this weather."

"Thanks, Gram." I turned towards the stairs. "Hey, where's Ollie?"

From the living room, a small voice chimed. "I'm over here."

I peeked around the corner. On the floor, propped in a circle around Olivia, stood G.I. Joe, Barbie, the Transformer with missing appendages, and now a fourth figure—poor Buster, wearing a red towel like a canine Superman. Buster thumped his tail when he saw me, but Ollie waved a chopstick at him like a sergeant major leading her troops. "Stay, Buster."

She resumed her session. "Okay. Once again, Barbie. Why are you unhappy with Joe?" Ollie, dishing out therapy like a junior Dr. Phil. Jeez. The kid watched way too much TV.

I dashed upstairs, minutes to go before meeting Simon. I threw a t-shirt, jacket and jeans into my backpack and tore down the hall. As I passed Gramps' door, I did a double take. The door was open just a crack—unusual since Gram always kept it closed. I slipped inside. Uneven footprints, larger than mine, circled the carpet, to the desk, and then back to the door again.

Fortier.

I searched the desk and relaxed when I found the photos and letter to the bank tucked inside the drawer, just as I had left them. I stuffed them into my backpack, then tore the sketches dated August 12 from the sketchbook and packed them too.

As I turned to go, Gramps' reading glasses caught my eye. I thought of him again, the way his life ended, the worry his disappearance caused Gram. Tom Hendricks had vanished. Gramps had gone missing. What if something happened to me too? Gram would worry all over again. I couldn't do that to her.

I rummaged through the desk for paper and an envelope. I scribbled a note, popped it into the envelope and sealed it. I fled down the stairs, skidding into the living room just as Olivia ended her therapy session with her new but used friends. "Ollie," I whispered.

"I need you to do something for me."

She eyed the backpack suspiciously. "Where are you going?"

"I'm having a sleep-over with Simon." Not exactly true, but close.

"Can I come?"

"I don't know. Maybe we'll go fishing for crayfish. We might even catch a few gophers. Do you like crayfish-gopher stew, Ollie?" It was a bald-faced lie, but tacking the word "maybe" in front of it made me feel a little less guilty.

Olivia turned pale. "That's okay. I changed my mind."

I handed Olivia the envelope. "Would you hang on to this for me and give it to Gram if I don't make it home by the time Mom and Dad get here?

"What's in it?"

"Nothing important. A letter."

Olivia examined the envelope, front and back. "Well...."

I threw in a bargaining chip, an offer I knew Olivia couldn't possibly refuse. "If you do, I'll take you to the tree house later. You'd like that wouldn't you?"

You'd think I'd just offered her a tour of Willy Wonka's chocolate factory. Olivia beamed and hugged me. "You will? Well, okay then."

"Remember, only give the envelope to Gram if I don't make it back on time tomorrow."

Finally free of his duties in Olivia's therapy session, Buster circled my legs, red cape dragging along the floor. I bent over, patted his neck and whispered, "I wish I could take you along."

Buster gazed at me, tongue lolling from his mouth like a pink necktie. He woofed and gave me his paw to shake as if to say, go ahead Nate. Do what you have to do. I'll wait.

I shook Buster's paw and hugged him hard. "I'll be back, boy. I promise."

In the kitchen, Gram and Fortier sat at the table, each nursing a cup of coffee. I glanced at the wall clock. Minutes I couldn't spare ticked away. "I'll see you tomorrow, Gram."

Gram pulled me closer and looked into my eyes. "You be careful, Nate."

I shrugged. "It's just a sleepover."

"I know, but I worry. You know I always do."

I hugged Gram. Over her shoulder, I saw Fortier, blue-grey eyes staring, his mouth in a lop-sided sneer. I looked away, to the window he'd just cleaned. Fortier turned to look too.

Puffy clouds drifted across the sky. A light drizzle replaced the fierce downpour.

"Storm's almost over." Fortier slurped his coffee. "Got to get going soon."

CHAPTER 17

Simon stood by the front door tapping his foot and holding a multi-coloured beach umbrella above his head.

"Wha-took-ya so long?"

Around his waist, Simon wore a belt strung with supplies—Swiss army knife, can opener, coil of rope, pair of pliers, flashlight. Over his shoulders, he carried the world's biggest backpack—so stuffed it looked ready to pop its seams.

"You have the kitchen sink in there too?" I asked.

"Just being prepared. You never know."

"You call your dad?"

"Yeah"

"And?"

"I told him I was sleeping over at your grandmother's. He's okay with it."

"Ditch the umbrella. It's hardly raining anymore. Besides, don't you have enough to carry already? You know…kitchen sink and all?"

Simon left the umbrella by the door, shifted the giant backpack to his other shoulder and pulled a cell phone out of his pocket. He held it at arm's length. "Smile."

"Are you going to be doing this the whole time?"

"It's a treasure hunt, right? Never know. National Geographic might want photos."

We synchronized our watches. Time was everything and we had little of it. The Greyhound bus left in just over an hour and we still had to find a way to the terminal, clear across town. But there was one more thing we needed to take care of. We couldn't risk Fortier getting to Paradise before us.

When I told Simon what we had to do, he freaked out. "Are you nuts?"

"It's the only way."

We wound through the hedge, through Gram's yard, and over to Fortier's house.

"Are you nuts?' Simon repeated a half-dozen times.

While Simon stood guard, I opened the garage door. It squawked and squealed along the track, and seemed even louder than before.

"Hurry, will ya?" Simon begged.

The car was locked, the trunk closed, with the canoe strapped to the roof, ready for Fortier's trip.

I searched through tools on the workbench and located a flat-head screwdriver. Dropping to my knees, I jammed the screwdriver into the valves of a front tire. Air hissed from the tire. It sagged then slowly crumpled into a rubbery puddle on the garage floor. I scurried to the next tire and then the others until they were all flat.

"Hurry up!" Simon called.

I unscrewed the license plates, dropped the screwdriver onto Fortier's workbench, and scanned the garage. Did Fortier have a compressor? If he did, he'd re-inflate the tires before our bus even passed the outskirts of the city. I relaxed a bit when I couldn't find one. Perfect.

Simon rounded the corner. "Come on. We'll never make—" He saw me holding the license plates. "Jeez, Nate."

I hid one of the license plates inside a box containing bottles of motor oil, and the other inside a cupboard filled with paint cans. "That should slow the old goat down."

"Ah...um...look, Nate." Simon pointed at the cupboard with a trembling hand.

I followed his gaze to a poster taped to the inside of the cupboard door. A familiar face stared back at me along with a message.

WANTED FOR ARMED ROBBERY

Simon's mouth fell open. "Isn't that Farter?"

I looked closer. "Oh, my God."

The man in the photo looked about twenty years old, but take away Fortier's wrinkles, replace the grey hair with black, tighten up the bags under his eyes, and he would be a near perfect match to the face on the poster. The criminal next door. Gramps had been right.

Simon pulled on my arm. "Let's get out of here before he comes back." He turned to run, then stopped abruptly.

"What are you doing?"

He ripped the poster down and jammed it into his hoodie pocket. "You never know when it might come in handy."

We fled the garage just as Gram's door opened.

"See you in a few days, Mildred," a raspy voice called.

We ran down the street, hearts pounding like the devil was after us, but laughing like crazy. I pictured Fortier's reaction as he rounded the corner. Too bad we wouldn't be there to see it.

CHAPTER 18

Frenzied activity took up the next forty-five minutes. Dashing to the corner to catch the transit bus. Transferring to another. Arriving at the Greyhound terminal. Racing to the ticket counter with just minutes to spare—

"Yes?" the man at the ticket counter said briskly. "Can I help you?" Like the buses, he seemed to be on a tight schedule.

"We'd like two tickets to Paradise." I dumped a pile of bills and loose coins on the counter.

The ticket agent, a little balding man with raisin-like eyes, studied me then looked at Simon. "How old are you?" he asked.

According to the Greyhound website, children fourteen and under required someone older to travel with them on the bus.

Simon stretched himself to his full height which brought him almost up to my armpit.

"I'm almost thirteen," he announced proudly.

The man's raisin eyes narrowed. "You sure don't look it."

"He is." I straightened my shoulders and deepened my voice to seem older. "I can vouch for him." I checked the clock above the ticket booth. "Please sir. We'll miss our bus if we don't hurry."

The agent muttered something under his breath that sounded like, "Darn kids. What's the world coming to?" He tapped a few keys on the computer and presented us with two tickets. "Gate Four. Better run."

At the gate, the security officer eyed my backpack and waved me on, but when he spotted Simon's giant one, he put up his hand. "Hold it, kid. Way too big. It's gotta go in the baggage compartment below."

"Aw, gee," Simon muttered. As he dropped his backpack, his supply belt clattered, attracting stares from everyone around.

"That goes below too," the officer said. "No dangerous goods aboard. Security's tight these days, you know."

Simon's face drooped, but as soon as he stepped on the bus, his disappointment vanished. "Back two rows are empty, Nate. Race ya!"

While Simon slid into the window seat, I stashed my backpack on the seat behind.

The Greyhound rolled out of the bus depot on schedule. Fifteen minutes later, it rumbled along the Trans Canada Highway past fields of waving wheat.

Simon broke into a fit of laughter.

"What's so funny?" I said.

"Farter."

I laughed too. "Yeah, beauty."

We high fived and killed ourselves with more laughter, only stopping when a large woman in front of us turned around to shoot an evil stare. I imagined Fortier's reaction—the stunned look on his face the moment he saw the car. Seconds of silence as he stood there, mouth wide open. The slow blooming expression of anger as he realized just what had happened—and the rant of cuss words to follow.

Beautiful, just beautiful.

Simon grabbed my arm, serious for a moment. "You think that was Farter on the poster?"

"Sure looked like him."

"Do you think he robbed a bank? Maybe he's still on the run. Maybe there's a reward for his capture." Simon rattled with excitement. "Do you think we should turn him in?"

"Whoa, get a grip. We don't know anything. Besides we've got enough on our plates already."

Still, Simon's outburst started me thinking. If Fortier was a bank robber on the run that would explain so much—his interest in the gold, skulking about Gram's house, all the attention to Gram. For the first time, I worried for Gram's safety, alone and helpless, living next door to a man she obviously trusted. A man on a wanted poster.

The bus stopped at every small town along the way. Some passengers got off. New ones boarded to take their place. At one depot, a man reeking of cigarettes slid into the seat in front of us.

Simon wrinkled his nose. "Yuck. What's that smell?"

I elbowed him. "Shh."

"What?" Simon said, clueless of my embarrassment. "What?"

Fortunately, Simon nodded off soon after and I was gifted with a few minutes of silence.

I hauled out the map, studied it again, and traced our route as the bus rumbled along the highway. When the bus pulled into the town of Minnedosa, the cigarette smoker left, giving us the luxury of having the back rows to ourselves again.

"Where are we?" Simon mumbled. He nodded off again before I could answer.

Police found Gramps somewhere near Minnedosa, perhaps along this very road. Had he been heading to Paradise as I suspected? Was he carrying the shovel to dig up the long lost gold?

Gradually, the scenery changed. Bald prairie disappeared, replaced by slopes flanked with trees and scrub brush. The bus dipped around tight curves and climbed steep hills. Up, down, around. The engine worked harder—like an athlete finally breaking into a sweat.

An hour past Minnedosa, the bus rumbled into Paradise and stopped at a gas station that doubled as the town's bus depot.

I shook Simon. "Come on. This is where we get off."

He jolted awake. "Wha…We're here? Already?" Simon, eyes still half-closed, stumbled down the aisle ahead of me.

After Simon retrieved his backpack and supply belt from the baggage compartment, we stood on the sidewalk and watched the bus disappear with a roar down the main street.

Simon took another selfie and glanced around. "So this is Paradise."

We made quite the pair, one tall kid with a small backpack, a shorter kid carrying an oversized one, two souls in a town with a heavenly name that, as it turned out, was nothing at all like paradise.

CHAPTER 19

"Staying a while?" a voice asked. It came from the gas jockey, a scrawny, unshaven guy a few years older than me. He chewed a thick wad of gum, forcing it aside with his tongue whenever he spoke.

"Maybe," I said.

"Visiting relatives here, are you?" the man asked, as if he couldn't possibly think of any other reason someone would stop in Paradise. "Well, you two have a good time." He turned and vanished inside the gas station.

I stood beside Simon and listened to the fading hum of the bus as it hit the highway on the outskirts of town. I checked my watch. Seven. "Come on, Simon. Let's look around."

We strolled down the main street—an awfully short trip. In less than ten minutes, we walked the full length of the street. We crossed to the other side and walked back. There wasn't much to see. A wooden white-washed church on one corner, a deserted old lumber mill on another, and between them a few shops and other buildings: a hair salon, grocery store, coffee shop and a two-storey stone structure that served as the town hall, library and museum. Other buildings were empty, their windows boarded over.

"Pretty pathetic town, isn't it?" Simon said.

We trudged along the main street again, this time more slowly and carefully. Simon, hunched over like a troll hauling a heavy load, wheezed with each step.

"Want to trade?" I said. "I'll carry yours if you like."

"I'm okay." Beads of sweat trickled down his face. Wet spots circled the armpits of his t-shirt.

"You sure? You look like you're going to pass out."

"I'm fine. Really."

We peered into windows, poked our heads into shops, and read each overhead sign. At the town hall, we noticed several posters plastered on a window. *Halt Hydro. Preserve Your History. Conserve Nature.*

"Wonder what that's about?" I asked.

Simon's face was the colour of a ripe tomato. "Dunno. Don't care," he wheezed, plowing on.

Even at our slow pace, we arrived back at the gas station in fifteen minutes. Simon collapsed on a bench and wiped the sweat off his forehead. "Maybe we missed something."

"Yeah, maybe."

We searched the town again, this time meandering along gravel side roads sparsely sprinkled with houses, about thirty in all, some well tended, others tired and worn. A few teetered on the brink of collapse.

Simon plodded a pace behind me, his shoes kicking up swirls of dust.

"You okay?" I asked.

"Yeah."

But there was less enthusiasm in Simon's voice now, less bounce in his step, and his supply belt hung so low that the flashlight scraped the ground.

We reached the end of town and wandered the main street again. The pavement, baked for hours now, magnified the heat. Suddenly it was all too much for Simon—the backpack cutting into his shoulders, the sweat swimming down his cheeks, the stifling heat sucking life from his body. In combination they delivered a knock-out punch. Simon's legs buckled, his body folded. Down he went.

Just before Simon hit the sidewalk, I grabbed him. Right then, food, water and rest seemed more important than gold, more urgent than finding lost treasure.

CHAPTER 20

Simon looked like wilted lettuce, long past its expiry date.

"Let me help." I grabbed his backpack and slung it over my shoulder.

"Thangsh," Simon mumbled, clutching my arm for support.

We stumbled to the coffee shop and slipped inside. Blinds darkened the windows, probably to seal out the heat. A ceiling fan whirred above, blowing cool air over us. While my eyes adjusted to the dark, Simon lingered under the fan, face upturned, arms outstretched.

"That feels so good," he said, soaking up the breeze.

While Simon recovered, I tried to get my bearings. Deep in the dark coffee shop, three men hunched around one table, hardy types with leather-like skin, heavy into an argument. At another table, two chatty ladies held forks over plates of pie. Between the tables, a lone waitress shuttled coffee across the black-and-white tiled floor.

We tossed our backpacks into a corner booth and slid across the vinyl upholstery.

Simon fumbled with the menu. "I can't see a thing," he whined.

"Forget the menu. Just order what you always do."

The waitress plunked two glasses of ice water on the table. "What'll it be, boys?"

We ordered burgers, fries and soft drinks.

"Make mine an extra large." Simon slugged back water like it was the last bit of moisture on earth. He rebounded quickly. He opened the blinds to banish some of the dark. While we waited for our meals, he built a tower out of sugar cubes and creamers.

I closed my eyes, tired and hungry, but more than anything, discouraged and disappointed. What idiots we'd been to risk everything on such a crazy scheme. Other than the advertising flyer, no evidence existed that Gramps ever visited Paradise. We'd taken a bus to no-where. There wouldn't be another bus until tomorrow. Now we were stranded in this run-down town, a town so tiny it didn't even have a school or motel.

"Okay. Here you go." The waitress planted plates loaded with ham-burgers and fries in front of us and a bottle of ketchup in the middle.

Simon grabbed a fistful of fries and shoveled them into his mouth.

"Dude," the waitress said to me, "you're awfully pale. Are you all right?"

For the first time, I looked closely at her. She was sixteen, maybe sev-enteen, and had the most perfect face—oval-shaped with milky white skin, cherry-red lips, and sparkling green eyes. Earrings dangled from beneath shoulder-length, curly black hair. She wore blue jeans and a crisp, short-sleeved white shirt pinned with a large button that said *Stop the Flooding*. Tattoos of vines and flowers crawled up her arms. A heart on her right bicep held a single word: Timmy.

"Are you okay?" she asked again.

"Yeah," I dropped my gaze. "I guess the heat just got to me."

"Awful, isn't it?"

I looked at Simon. He sat frozen in mid-chew, his stare locked on the waitress, speechless for the first time in his life.

The waitress studied us. "So. You just get into town? From the city, right?"

Was it that obvious? In the city, no one noticed strangers, but in small towns like Paradise everyone probably knew everyone in town. New people must stand out from the rest. They begged questions.

"Yeah, we're from Winnipeg," I said. I wasn't sure how much de-tail to provide, but the waitress with the perfect face and sympathetic green eyes seemed to want more. "We just came in on the bus."

"So you'll be staying a while, then?"

"A while. Till tomorrow."

The waitress eyed Simon's overstuffed backpack. If she was the least bit curious, she didn't let on. "Well, welcome to Paradise. My name is Marnie."

"I'm Nate and this—"

"I'm Simon." With a ketchup-smeared smile, Simon reached over to pump Marnie's hand, almost dumping his soda. "Pleased to meet ya."

"Nice to meet you both too." Marnie spun around and headed back to the counter.

I downed the hamburger and fries. The food and drink worked their magic. Energy gradually returned. Dark feelings vanished, and hope made a slow but steady comeback.

Simon rested his head on his hand, watching Marnie pour coffee at another table. "She's beautiful, isn't she?"

"Snap out of it, Simon. We're not here to stare at pretty girls." I dragged out the photographs, sketches and map out of my backpack and spread them on the table. "Come on. We've got to figure this out." What had we missed? We studied Gramps' map again.

"There's Paradise," Simon said helpfully. "There's Shipment #35."

"Look," I said, stabbing the map to make my point. "They're not exactly at the same place. They're a tiny bit apart."

"So?"

"So, given the scale of the map, it means the two places are farther away from each other than we originally thought. Maybe the gold isn't in Paradise after all."

"Looks like serious stuff," a soft voice said.

I looked up to see Marnie standing by my side, water pitcher in hand. She scanned the papers on the table. Although Marnie hadn't asked a question, her green eyes begged for more information.

My brain said *no*. Stop. Don't say more. Be cautious.

Apparently Simon's brain operated by different rules. "They belonged to Nate's grandfather," he gushed. "We're not sure what it means, but—"

I kicked Simon under the table.

"Ow. What's your problem, Nate?"

"Hey, Marnie," one of the squabbling men hollered.

Marnie grabbed the coffee pot off the counter and headed to their table.

"You can't go telling everyone about the gold," I hissed at Simon. "You want the whole town searching for it?"

"She looks pretty trustworthy," Simon grumbled. Then he pouted for a full ten seconds—a new record for him. "She's awfully sweet," he said at last.

Marnie put the coffee pot back on the counter and returned to our table. "These are your grandfather's, right?"

I nodded.

Before I could protest, Marnie slid into the seat beside Simon. "This," she picked up the photograph of the lake surrounded by trees. "This is Whitewater Lake. I'm positive it is." She reached across the table and sifted through the papers. "Okay. Now I'm definitely curious." She held up the photograph of old buildings I'd found in Gramps' desk. "Do you know what this is?"

I shook my head.

"This is the old Whitewater camp, about eight kilometres north of town. Not much of it left now. Most of it was demolished in the 1940s." Marnie looked at me closely. "Why would your grandfather be interested in Whitewater Lake and the old camp?"

Simon started to say something. I kicked him again and fired a warning look.

Simon glared and kicked me back.

Marnie's questions hung in the air. Mentally, I rattled through a list of possible answers, all lies.

"Hey, Marnie. More coffee."

Marnie sighed and headed for the coffee pot.

Whew! Saved by three men arguing. I scooped up the papers and stuffed them into my backpack. "Come on, Simon. Let's go."

"Can't we stay here?"

I slapped enough money on the table to cover the bill and a tip. I liked Marnie and trusted her as much as anyone could a stranger they'd known for all of thirty minutes, but I didn't trust her enough to tell her the whole story.

Simon struggled with his backpack, whining the whole while. "Can't we just stay here?"

Just then the door opened. A woman entered, followed by a man. Even in the dim light, their uniforms were unmistakable. RCMP officers.

I froze. Were they looking for us?

CHAPTER 21

The RCMP officers approached Marnie. Their backs were turned and the squabbling men drowned out their conversation.

"Come on, Simon." I pushed him to the door. His supply belt clanged as we edged past the officers, but they were so involved in their discussion with Marnie they didn't seem to notice.

"When did you see them?" I heard one ask.

Pinprick stabs raced up my arm. We scurried out the door, stepped into sunshine, and fled down the street.

"What was that all about?" Simon asked.

I checked my watch. Eight-fifteen. Who knew we were missing— and in Paradise of all places?

"Fortier," I said more to myself than Simon.

"What?"

I shoved Simon into the doorway of an abandoned building and looked back down the street. "Fortier. Do you think he might have figured it out? That we're here, I mean?"

"Well...." Simon scratched his head and smiled. "He must've been awfully mad."

Luscious memories of flattened tires and missing license plates returned. I punched Simon's shoulder. "Bet that slowed him down."

He punched me back. "Wish I'd been there."

We punched each other a half dozen times and laughed so hard that I felt sick.

An RCMP cruiser tore past. We melted into the doorway again, jolted back to reality.

"So now what?" I said. "Fortier's probably on his way, and it's going to be dark soon. We can't stay here."

We walked down back roads, lost in thoughts of our own. By the time we reached the gas station, a new plan had emerged from the ashes of the old one. "Whitewater Lake," I announced.

"Huh?"

"Marnie said that's where the photos were taken. The gold's not here. Maybe it's there."

"Maybe."

The gas station was still open. Simon bee lined to the candy display, leaving me to question the gum-chewing gas jockey myself.

"Could you tell me how to get to Whitewater Lake?"

The gas-jockey pushed the wad of gum into his cheek and sucked back a mouthful of spit before he spoke. "Whitewater Lake? There's an old logging road that runs behind the lumber mill at the edge of town. It goes to Whitewater Lake. It's not much of a road—more like a wide trail—hardly ever used anymore, but, yeah, that's your best bet."

"Is the old camp along that road?"

He gulped and swallowed spit. "The old Whitewater camp? Yep. About eight kilometres down. Right beside the lake. Thinking about going there, are you?" He stooped to tidy up the display counter, leaving the question hanging.

I found Simon holding a fistful of chocolate bars and ogling a bucket of lollipops. "Come on. Put those down. We've got to get moving," I said.

As we rushed out of the gas station, the gas jockey called, "If you're going to that camp, you'll have to hurry. It'll be dark soon."

CHAPTER 22

To bypass the coffee shop, we ran along a deserted back lane to the edge of town. The old lumber mill stood there, a huge tottering structure of rotting wood and peeling paint. The smell of sawdust lingered in the air. Behind the mill, we found the old logging road, dotted with loose gravel and deep ruts, but still passable.

We'd been wrong. The gold wasn't in Paradise after all, but probably at Whitewater Lake, down a pitted road that cut through the forest and led to an old camp. With darkness only an hour away, we set off at a brisk pace, like two explorers on a great adventure. The sun shifted west, covering much of the old road with shade. We dipped into cool shadows, dodged ruts and avoided stones, determined to reach the old camp by nightfall.

At first Simon chatted excitedly and took selfies at every turn. But running with the heavy backpack quickly took a toll. He quieted and fell behind, puffing like a steam engine.

"Come on, Simon."

"Go ahead. I'll catch up," he wheezed.

I marched on, focused on the road ahead. The twisted, uneven trail snaked over hills and through the forest. The road leading to Whitewater Lake, to Gramps' shipment of gold, to the treasure he kept secret from Gram. With each step, I thought of her too—her worry on Gramps last day, the loneliness she felt now. And then there was Fortier—a known criminal, always lurking around Gram, going on a fishing trip that didn't exist. What was it Simon called him? A snake, a low-down, dirty, rotten, no good....

Just where was Fortier? Likely on his way by now, hopping mad with tires re-inflated and license plates secured. If only we hadn't wasted almost an hour at the coffee shop.

A bird flew across the road, jarring me out of my thoughts.

Simon.

Far behind, in the gathering darkness, a tiny hunched-over figure plodded toward me, leaving a wake of dust. "You can do it, Simon," I shouted, waving him on. "It can't be much farther." I waited by the side of the road. As the gap between us closed, I shouted encouragement. "Way to go. Nice work, Simon."

He smiled, but weighed down with the heavy pack, each step seemed a monumental burden.

From deep in the forest, sounds echoed between the clang and clatter of Simon's belt. The snap of a twig. The sad song of a loon. Sounds of night approaching. Then something mechanical. The purr of an engine. The crunch of tires on gravel. The blare of a radio.

A car.

"Quick, Simon." I ran to him, grabbed his arm, and dragged him behind a thicket.

"What the heck are you doing?" Simon voice sounded thin, sort of like a wheezing Miss Piggy.

"Be quiet, will you? It might be Fortier."

"Farter? No way."

A small blue car rounded the curve and slowed as it neared us.

"Whew. Not Fortier," I said.

So much dust layered the windows that I couldn't make out the driver. The car stopped. The driver's window opened. Rock music blasted through the forest. An oval face appeared, milky white skin and sparkling green eyes framed by shoulder-length, curly black hair.

"It's Marnie," Simon yelled.

I clamped my hand over Simon's mouth and pulled him closer. "Not a word."

Marnie climbed out of the car. "Nate? Simon? I know you're here." She wandered down the road, peered into the bushes and called our names again. She passed within inches of our hiding place—which sent Simon into a frenzy of squirming—but I held on tight.

"Shhh. She can't know we're here."

Marnie returned to her car, gunned the engine and drove off.

The moment I released Simon, he ran to the road, waving furiously. But Marnie's car roared away, a swirling cloud in the distance. Simon wailed. "Why'd you do that?"

"This was Gramps secret. Now it's ours. She's a complete stranger. We don't know if we can trust her."

We started down the road again, but within minutes a blue dot appeared on the horizon. I grabbed Simon in a bear hug and ducked behind a tree. No struggles this time.

Marnie slowed down, stuck her head out the window and scanned the bushes. Then she drove off, radio booming, spewing gravel as she gunned it back toward town.

Simon shook me off, adjusted his backpack and stormed ahead. "We could have used her help," he muttered.

I passed him in a few steps. "Give me your backpack. I'll carry them both."

Simon glared at me. "Don't bother."

"We'll be there soon. It can't be much farther."

"Yeah, like you haven't said that before." Simon forged on, kicking stones. "She might have helped," he griped.

The sun dipped below the trees; only minutes of daylight left. "We'll never get there at this rate." I threw up my hands in disgust and ran, knowing that Simon would never let me get far. Sure enough, when I looked back, Simon was galloping full tilt, supply belt swaying and clattering.

In a race against nightfall, I barreled down the road. My feet clipped ruts and hollows, rounded turns, dipped into long shadows and steered into sunny patches again. Along one stretch, the road curved, veered across a bald patch of prairie and turned directly into the setting sun. I ran, wrapped in a brilliant haze, unable to see the road or my own feet.

An eerie feeling washed over me. I had been here before. In this place. Running along a rutted road through light so dazzling I could barely see. In my dream, it had been just like this. I stopped.

Simon trotted up a moment later. "Why'd you stop?"

"It's here, Simon."

"What's here?"

I motioned to the bushes at the side of the road. "That."

CHAPTER 23

Beside the road, partly hidden by brush, a battered sign announced *Whitewater Camp: Straight Ahead.*

"Lucky find." Simon snapped a selfie. "Would be easy to miss."

"Yeah. Lucky." But I knew it wasn't really luck. Gramps brought me here. I spied a second sign, almost covered by bushes: *Evacuation Order.* Below the title, in fine print, a few paragraphs provided details.

"What's it say?" Simon asked.

I moved closer, squinting, but in the growing darkness the tiny print was impossible to read.

"Wait." Simon fumbled with his supply belt and unclipped the flashlight. "Here."

"Never mind," I said. "We better keep moving."

A path ran from the road into the woods. Only a thin slit of sunlight remained and the moon rose full and bright across the blue-black sky.

"This way." Simon waved the flashlight and charged ahead.

In the moonlight, trees took on grotesque shapes, and roots wiggled like snakes across the weed-choked path. At first, Simon pointed out each weird figure like he was some kind of tour guide, but when a wolf howled, Simon stopped.

"Ah...," he said. His hand shook as he passed the flashlight to me. "Maybe you should go first."

Not more than a hundred metres from the road, Simon's belt snagged on a large jagged rock, forcing us to stop. I shone the light on it. The rock looked oddly out of place—pebbly-looking, gnarled, and more man-made than natural.

"That's not a rock. More like concrete, don't you think?" I said.

Simon pointed ahead. "Look there's another one over there. Wow!"

He tossed his backpack aside, grabbed the flashlight out of my hands and raced across the clearing, tripping over roots and stones.

"Simon," I called. "There's no way we'll make it back to Paradise for the night." Too dark to see much, I stayed behind rather than risk wandering off the trail. "Simon, come back."

An owl hooted. That started an avalanche of sounds—crickets chirping, frogs croaking, and off in the distance, a choir of wolves howling. In no time, Simon was back, cringing at my side.

"Quit fooling around," I told him. "We have to find a place to sleep."

Near one of the concrete blocks, a few logs crisscrossed into an A-shape over a dip in the ground. "There. That's a good spot for a shelter."

"There," Simon repeated. "Wait. I've got the perfect thing."

He rummaged through the backpack, pulled out a small axe, and started chopping branches off a nearby aspen tree.

"Hope you brought a first aid kit too," I said.

While Simon chopped, I hauled cut branches to the site. Together, we layered them over the dip in the ground and weaved them between the crisscrossed logs. In fifteen minutes, we had a rickety shelter, just high enough to sit up straight under and just long enough that we could stretch out to lie down.

"You wouldn't happen to have something to eat in there, would you?" I said as Simon wedged his backpack through the narrow opening. Hours had passed since our meal in the coffee shop and I was ravenous.

Simon dug through the backpack, pulled out a coffee pot, a raincoat, rubber boots, Batman underwear and a matching Robin t-shirt.

"It's here somewhere," he said. "I know I packed it."

Other strange objects surfaced–magnifying glass, electrical wire, duct tape, scissors, plastic tarp....

"Hey, I forgot I'd packed these." Simon threw a small rectangular object to me. In the dark, I couldn't tell exactly what it was. The object crackled and sputtered. "Breaker, breaker...Simon calling Nate. Over."

"Walkie-talkies? You're kidding!"

"Come on, Nate. Pick it up."

I rolled my eyes and picked up the walkie-talkie. "Nate to Simon. I'm starving. Find me something to eat. Over."

"Oh, yeah. I forgot."

Simon dug into the backpack again and held up a huge baggie of squished and mangled sandwiches. "See, told you I had something."

We munched on sticky peanut butter and jam sandwiches, and washed them down with crushed drinking boxes Simon found at the bottom of the backpack. For dessert, Simon tossed me a bruised apple and a bag of chips. Later we scooped up dry leaves, shaped piles of them into cushy pillows and gathered others to make fluffy mattresses.

Simon stretched out on his bed, arms behind his head. "Ain't this the life," he said.

I spread the tarp over us like a blanket. The moon hung over the quiet forest like a lonely light bulb in the black sky. We were far from home in a makeshift shelter, in the thick of a strange forest. Alone. Just the two of us.

The wolves howled again, closer this time. Simon pulled up the tarp. Only his eyes showed above it. Despite the heat, he shivered.

"Simon, we're going to be alright. Really."

"I know." His voice sounded tiny and hollow. "I know."

I thought of our tree house campout. "Remember the last time we slept outside?" I asked.

"You were scared silly."

"I was scared? You were the one bawling and screaming."

We erupted in laughter and punched each other soundly. "Guess this isn't all that different," Simon said.

"No, I guess it isn't."

Moments later, Simon's breathing turned soft. He must've fallen asleep. The forest grew even more quiet.

Suddenly, a stiff breeze slipped through the trees, rustling leaves and sweeping cool relief into the shelter. In an instant, the wind died and everything stilled. Just like what happened during the garage sale. The wild wind started me on this journey and now, here in this strange place, it offered encouragement. All at once, I felt at ease. Gramps again, letting me know I was doing the right thing.

I tossed around for a while to find a comfortable position, but finally, overcome by exhaustion, I fell asleep.

The crunch of twigs woke me up. Framed in the bright moonlight, a dark shadow lumbered past the shelter. I sat up. My heart hammered against my ribs. My stomach churned. I checked my glow-in-the-dark watch. One a.m.

Something snorted—an animal searching for food? A foul stench arose, along with grunts and heavy thuds along the ground. A bear. It had to be a bear!

Simon rolled over, still asleep. I couldn't see the animal, but I heard it thrash closer and closer. I patted the ground quietly to locate the plastic bag with its enticing peanut butter sandwiches, but couldn't find it.

Don't breathe. Don't move. Pray it goes away.

Ages later, the heavy footsteps ebbed. Once more, the forest grew calm. Again I heard Simon's soft breathing. Certain the animal had gone, I relaxed. I dozed fitfully with an ear on the forest, wary of sounds that signalled the creature's return.

I slipped into a dream.

I run through blinding light down a rutted road. When the glare lifts, I follow a narrow trail choked with weeds and roots. I enter a clearing surrounded by thick forest and dotted with wooden buildings built of thick vertical planks.

I'm not alone. Dozens of men mill around me. One man leads the group, taller than the others, his stride confident and strong. I can't see his face clearly, not at first, but I know who he is. There is no mistaking the broad shoulders, the square jaw, the patch of stubborn hair sticking straight up.

CHAPTER 24

Under the blaze of the rising sun, our makeshift shelter turned into a sauna. I woke up cloaked in sweat with a fist-sized knot throbbing in my back. I peeled off the tarp, stretched my cramped legs and checked the ground. No wonder I hurt—I'd slept on a twisted root the whole night.

Simon tore out of the shelter and headed into the bush to pee. I crawled out, stumbled a few wobbly steps and found my own spot. By daylight, the clearing looked peaceful and calm. Had I imagined the bear's visit?

"Nate, take a look at this."

Simon stood beside a tree only a few metres from our shelter. Claw marks raked the trunk. Grass, matted and crushed, ringed the base. "Hey, neat." He pointed to a heap of fresh droppings, the bear's parting gift.

"Right. Bear poop. Just what everybody wants to find when they're camping."

We shared another mangled sandwich and a bag of cheese noodles. While Simon explored the site, I searched for suitable weapons. Using Simon's axe, I hacked a branch from a small tree, stripped off the bark and rounded the end.

"What's that?" Simon asked.

"A club." I waved the weapon and practiced my moves. "You know, in case the bear comes back."

Simon imitated my moves, delivering imaginary blows. "I didn't know you were such a bear expert."

"Well, I'm not really. But like you always say, it never hurts to be prepared."

Simon bounded into the forest swinging the axe. Minutes later, he returned dragging a long, heavy branch. While he trimmed it, I took out the map, photos and other things of Gramps' and wandered the site. I scanned the wide, flat clearing. A creek bed sliced across the barren grassy field, dry now, but in spring or after a heavy rain, probably bubbling with life. Beyond the clearing, at the bottom of a gentle slope flanked with trees, Whitewater Lake's surface rippled in the morning light. All the ingredients for a camp were here: trees for shelter, a supply of fresh water, protection from wind and harsh weather, and a road nearby to carry supplies back and forth.

Simon joined me, looking like a cave man ready for battle. In one hand, he held a spear, sharpened to a pinprick point. In the other hand, a long club. Clipped to his supply belt, I noticed a new addition—a slim sword fashioned from branches, a handle secured with duct tape.

"You have more weapons than most armies," I said.

Simon flashed a bright smile. "Gee, thanks."

Guided by the photograph of old buildings, we explored the clearing. Little remained of the original camp, just a few concrete piles from the foundations. So disappointing.

I remembered the shovel in the trunk of Gramps' car. Had he been here?

"Look for upturned soil," I told Simon. "Signs of digging."

We located a few ant hills, dozens of gopher holes, and a small natural cavity on the side of a slope that might have been the bear's winter den. Nothing newly dug. Nothing large enough to hide a shipment of gold.

All along we watched for the downed plane. If it crashed near the camp, something of it should remain—the fuselage, a wing, the engine—something. But we found nothing. Not a single shred of twisted metal.

"Nate, look." Simon pointed to a hazy wisp of smoke spiraling over the forest not far from the lake. "Do you think it's him?"

"Might be."

A soft breeze fanned the smoke, breaking it into thin threads that curled above towering trees. "Farter," Simon said. "That no good, rotten…."

We hurried our search, wary now that we might run into Fortier. "Do you remember when the bus comes?" I asked.

"Hmm…five, I think."

I checked my watch. Ten o'clock in the morning and still no evidence, a discouraging fact given all the risks we'd taken. Our plan hinged on being a step ahead of Fortier and back home before anyone suspected a thing.

We followed the dry creek bed. At its mouth, where it emptied into the lake, a half-buried log protruded from the dirt. I recognized it— the missing bark, the hollow middle section, the curved ends. I sifted through Gramps' sketches and located the one of a decaying log.

"What you find?" Simon asked.

"Not exactly sure."

Walking in a circle, I compared the changing views. I stopped when the log before me matched the one in the sketch. I showed Simon. "See. It's the same. Gramps stood right here when he drew it."

Simon snapped another selfie and then we searched for other objects in Gramps' sketches. I made a game of it, racing against Simon to see who might pinpoint the exact spot where Gramps stood. From each position, we matched our view to the one drawn by Gramps. The rectangular object protruding from the ground turned out to be the largest of the concrete piles. The sketch of a gnarled tree? Made on top a knoll on the west side of the clearing.

"Spooky," Simon said. "Like your grandfather is here with us."

A haunting feeling crept through me, just like the one I felt in Gramps' car. I stood in Gramps' footsteps, seeing what he had seen. Gramps wanted me here. But why? A downed plane. A fortune in gold. We couldn't find a trace of either.

My gaze swept across a jog in the shoreline. A figure emerged from the woods—gimp legged, hobbling, and holding a book.

CHAPTER 25

Simon ducked behind a boulder and pulled me beside him. "Farter!" he whispered, pulling out his sword.

Wearing a red shirt and green pants, Fortier looked like an ad for Christmas. He limped along the shore, reading a small book. He stopped to gaze at the lake then resumed his slow walk. Where the shoreline curved, Fortier stopped again. He studied the book, shook his head, and wheeled around to stare at the forest.

"Hide," Simon hissed, yanking me down.

When we looked up seconds later, Fortier had retraced his steps. At the jog in the shoreline, he ventured into the woods and disappeared again.

I stuffed the sketches into my backpack. "Come on. Let's follow him."

"Are you nuts? Why?"

"He's here, isn't he?"

"So?"

"He's got the other box, remember?"

"So?"

"So, Fortier probably knows something about Shipment #35 that we don't." I glanced at my watch. "Look, it's almost noon. The bus leaves at five. We can't be late."

Simon crossed his arms and shook his head. "Go ahead if you want, but I'm staying right here."

Persuading Simon was a little like trying to reason with a cat. It took a whole lot of convincing. "We're spies, right?"

Simon's eyes narrowed. He kicked a stone, pinging it off the boulder. "Yeah, suppose so."

"Well, where are your walkie-talkies? Spies carry communication devices, don't they?"

Simon swung around, threw down the backpack and dug through it. A small mountain grew around his feet—tarp, underwear, an axe, electrical wire. "Got 'em!" He proudly held up the walkie-talkies and handed one to me.

Before I could turn it on, Simon bolted for the shoreline, swinging the sword with one hand and holding the walkie-talkie with the other. His overstuffed bag swayed from his shoulder.

"Wait up, Simon!" I yelled.

We circled the lake and followed the trail Fortier used earlier. It wound past an outcropping of rocks, crossed over a small hill, threaded through a dense grove of trees and ended in another clearing.

Simon froze. His mouth opened and closed like a fish gulping air. He pointed. Not more than twenty paces away, sitting on a stump beside a small tent, was Fortier. He tended a fire, looking sleazy like always. He threw on another log and prodded it with a stick. Flames shot higher, spewing embers into the sky. Heat from the blaze warmed my face.

I grabbed Simon's arm and jerked him off the trail. We hid behind a bush just before Fortier cranked around to look.

Simon popped his head above the leaves, then ducked. "The box! Take a look."

I peeked around the bush. This time I noticed a few details—a shovel, an axe and a metal tool box beside the stump. A cardboard box wrapped with masking tape at Fortier's feet. "*Garden Supplies*," I whispered.

Fortier stopped poking the fire and reached into the box. He pulled out a small black book and flipped through the pages. Then he stopped, stood, gazed across the forest, turned and looked toward the lake, then to the rocks, and back to the forest again. He sat down and returned to the book. He repeated that sequence several times—flipping, pausing, standing, scanning, sitting down again. "Bloody waste of time," he grumbled.

"What's he doing?" Simon hissed.

"Reading a book. No wait. He's getting up."

Fortier tossed the book into the cardboard box. He carried the box into the tent, then reappeared, picked up the axe, and sat on the stump again. From the tool box, Fortier selected a metal file.

"Now he's sharpening an axe."

"An axe?" Before I could stop him, Simon stood up. His backpack snagged on the bush. The supply belt clattered.

I grabbed Simon and pulled him down.

Fortier scrambled to his feet. "Who's there?" he boomed.

"Let's go," Simon screeched. He wrenched free and bolted like he'd been shot from a cannon.

Fortier charged, the axe still in his hand. "Come on. Show yourself."

I ran too, a few metres behind Simon. "Faster!" I screamed.

Simon tore through the underbrush, flying over weeds and stones, moving so fast I couldn't keep up.

A few dozen metres away, I glanced back. No sign of Fortier. I stopped. "Simon, wait up," I called.

But Simon kept running.

"Simon, come back. It's okay."

But he didn't stop.

"Calling Simon," I said over the walkie-talkie. "Come back. It's okay now. Over."

A winded voice answered. "You sure? Over."

"Yeah, I'm sure. Over."

A few minutes later, Simon returned, beet red and wheezing. He scanned the forest, looking as jittery as a mouse in a roomful of cats. "Where's Farter?" he asked.

"Good question."

We waited, ready to spring away if Fortier appeared. "We should go back to his camp," I said after a while.

"What? Why?"

"Because we don't know any more than we did before." I checked my watch. "We still haven't found the gold and Fortier knows something." I led the way back.

"Are you nuts?" Simon grumbled a few times. He quieted as we neared Fortier's camp. The fire still blazed, but there was no sign of the old man. "Lucky us," Simon said. He drew a deep breath. "Farter's not here. Can we go now?"

"Are you kidding?" I circled the fire and aimed for the tent. "This is our chance to investigate." I tore back the flap, about to enter, when I noticed a patch of red in the bushes behind. "What's this?" Peeling back the branches, I discovered Fortier, face down, sprawled like a rag doll on the ground. He wasn't moving.

"Maybe he's dead," said Simon. He sounded almost hopeful.

I turned Fortier over, checked for a pulse and found one—just barely. A jagged gash ran across his brow. Blood trickled down a rock under his head. "Not dead," I said. "Pretty banged up, though. He must have tripped."

Part of me wanted to leave Fortier. The old man had gotten what he deserved—justice served. But then I thought of Gramps dying by the road, alone in his car. No one deserved that. "Grab his legs, Simon."

"Are you nuts? I'm not touching him."

"Whatever." I grabbed Fortier under his arms and pulled.

Simon watched for a moment, then finally joined in. He muttered and complained as we dragged Fortier through the underbrush back to his campsite. Navigating Fortier into the small tent took a lot of heaving and shoving.

We rolled the old man on to his sleeping bag. Blood oozed from the gash, the skin around it already turning purple. I found a small towel in the tent and mopped up as much blood as possible. Fortier moaned. He turned his head. His eyes fluttered, then closed.

Simon bolted out of the tent.

"Relax," I said, calling him back. "He's still unconscious."

The cardboard box sat in the corner of the tent. *Garden Supplies.* I looked at Fortier. Out completely. Timing couldn't be better. I reached into the box and pulled out a drab blue shirt with a red circle on the back.

"Hey, just like the one you have," Simon said.

Actually, a few items were the same. Small buttons. A pipe. Another tin cup. But some items were unique too. Torn denim pants with a red stripe running down the leg. A small metal box engraved with weaving vines. A black book the size of a paperback, only thinner.

Simon edged closer. "Is that the one Farter was reading?"

"Maybe."

The book looked pretty battered, kind of like Fortier did now—tired and worn, a gash running across the leather cover, pages crumpled and yellow with age.

"What's it say?"

"I can't tell. A lot of pages are blank."

Fortier moaned. His hand flew up to his head. His eyes fluttered. "Wha...," he groaned.

Simon head jerked up. "Oh my God, he's coming to!"

He dashed out the tent, racing for his life. Not waiting a second more, I pocketed the book and fled after him. As we flew down the trail, a weak and garbled voice cried out. I had trouble making out the words.

"Wait! Wait!" Fortier seemed to be yelling.

Then again, he could have been saying something else. "Nate! Nate!" sounds pretty much the same.

CHAPTER 26

I caught up with Simon near the lake, bent over and gasping. "That was close. Now what?" he asked.

I shrugged. Fortier probably recognized us. He'd figure it out now, that we'd taken off, flattened his tires and hid the license plates, that we were searching for the gold just like him. Would he call Gram? Or the police? But why would he? Fortier had a criminal record. If he was after the gold, would he want a bunch of cops out here searching for Simon and me?

I thumbed through the book again. The cracked spine fell open in my hands. A few loose sheets almost blew away in the wind. I flipped past blank pages and others covered in scrawls too faint to read. I couldn't make out more than a word or two.

"Now what?" Simon asked again.

Smack in the center of the sky, the sun beat down relentlessly. The heat magnified my disappointment. We had no proof the gold was here, and soon we'd have to return to town, empty handed. "Maybe we missed something." I tried to keep a cheery outlook for Simon's sake. "Let's look around again."

We wandered to each spot in the sketches and examined every hill and knoll. I almost expected Fortier to appear, but he didn't. I smiled, imagining the giant headache he might be nursing.

Simon raced ahead. When he neared a clump of trees by the shoreline, he flung off his backpack and waved wildly. "I found something."

I ran to look, but by the time I got there, Simon had disappeared into the trees.

"Simon, where are you?"

"Down here," a small voice called. A head rose from a hole in the ground at the base of a tree, followed by a hand waving something that looked like a shredded license plate. Simon emerged, covered in dirt.

"What is it?"

Simon wiped the grimy object with his t-shirt and studied it for a long time. "Not sure, exactly. A chunk of metal. Aluminum judging by the way it bends easily. Something's stamped on it." He spat on the metal and scrubbed it again. "Looks like the letter N."

"Maybe. Could be M or Z."

"Or W. Do you think it's from the plane?"

"Maybe."

Our first real find! Whether it came from the plane or not, we were excited. We searched the clump of trees then wandered into shrubs thick with berries, hoping to locate other pieces.

"Wait." Simon hauled out his cell phone and held it above his head. "Gotta document this." He positioned the metal plate in front of his chest. "Wanna be in this one?"

I stood behind, squeezing close to fit in the picture.

"Ready. One…two…three. Say treasure!" Simon said. He checked the results. "That's a keeper."

"Yeah. Beauty!"

A far off cry caught our attention. I looked across the clearing, to the forest rimming the path to the road. A figure broke through the trees, running and waving—a girl. Dark curly hair, milky white skin.

Simon grinned. "Look, it's Marnie!"

Marnie pointed to the left. Then she waved again, furiously, with both arms this time.

Simon waved back without taking his eyes off of her. "Marnie!" he yelled. He yanked his backpack high onto his shoulder and ran to her, yelling gleefully.

I looked to the left, where Marnie pointed, and saw a dark hump moving through a berry thicket. Bear!

Marnie waved again and screamed. "Stop, Simon!"

But Simon plowed on, running a line directly past the berry patch and the bear. The bear swung its massive head, grunted, pawed the ground, and eyed Simon. Tiny berries or a whole meaty morsel?

Simon glanced over his shoulder. He saw the bear and froze.

"Don't stop, Simon. Run!" I yelled.

His mouth opened, then closed. Not a sound came out.

The bear charged toward us.

"Don't just stand there." I waved my club, screamed, and ran towards Simon. "Move it."

Simon found his feet and stormed ahead. I followed twenty paces behind. The bear charged through the thicket, past luscious berries, past fallen logs, through thick grass on the heels of its next meal—us.

"Run," Marnie yelled.

"Head to the concrete piles," I shouted to Simon.

To lighten my load, I dropped the backpack. Simon did the same. Somehow he loosened his belt too. Flashlight, Swiss army knife, can opener, coil of rope—even the wooden sword—slipped to the ground.

I sprinted on, not daring to look behind. When I spotted our shelter, I shouted directions. "Take cover here, Simon. Now!"

Simon dove through an opening between the logs. I leaped after him.

"Roll yourself into a ball. Tuck your legs underneath. Put your hands over your head."

Simon obeyed. I said a hasty prayer for the two of us. Then we waited, hands covering our heads, butts pointing up like sacrificial treats for the bear's pleasure.

CHAPTER 27

Seconds slipped by.

Simon peeked through his fingers. "What's happening?" he mouthed.

About ten metres away from us, the bear huffed and snorted. Through the branches of our shelter, we watched it attack Simon's backpack. With sharp teeth and claws, it mangled the coffee pot, shredded the blue tarp to ribbons, and ripped out the crotch of Simon's Batman underwear. The bear tossed a plastic baggie into the air and swallowed it in a single gulp. Simon's last sandwiches, gone in an instant. The bear sniffed around, downed a bag of chips, devoured a chocolate bar, and then, apparently satisfied with the meal, ambled toward the lake.

We waited until it vanished from sight before crawling out of our hiding spot.

"My stuff," Simon wailed.

"Stuff we can replace," I said. "At least we're still alive."

Seconds later, Marnie arrived, breathless from running. "You guys okay?"

Simon wiped away tears. Knees trembling, I picked up my backpack. Thankfully, it escaped the bear's wrath.

Simon stared at his backpack, shoulders slumped. Marnie put her arms around him. "Dude, you don't look so good."

We huddled around Simon's possessions. Fortunately, the damage was not as bad as we first thought. Simon's backpack was still usable, most of his things intact.

"See, Simon," Marnie said. "It's not so bad."

My rattled nerves settled. As my thoughts cleared, I remembered a few things.

#1: The Bus.

I looked at my watch. Three o'clock. Two hours until the bus would leave Paradise. We'd have to head for town soon.

#2: Fortier.

Where was he now?

#3: Marnie.

Why was she here?

"How did you know where we were?" I asked her. "Why did you come all the way here anyway?"

Marnie stooped to pick up Simon's underwear before answering. "Not many people come to Paradise. Few are teenagers carrying photographs of buildings at Whitewater Lake that disappeared long ago. I figured you'd be heading this way. What are you looking for?"

I kept quiet and studied my shoes.

"We're looking for gold!" Simon said, suddenly perky.

I frowned and glared at him. "Simon!"

Marnie hands flew to her hips. "Really. Gold?"

"Oh, I wasn't supposed to tell you," Simon said. "It's a secret."

"A secret? Really?"

"Simon!" I fired another warning look, but the blabbermouth continued.

"Nate's grandfather left a treasure map."

"I see. A treasure map. You sure?" Marnie looked at me, her green eyes flashing questions.

Once again I fell for Marnie's charm. I spilled my guts. I figured I didn't have much choice anyway, not with Simon shooting off his mouth. I talked about Gramps, the mislabelled box, the flyer linking him to Paradise, my discovery of the photos, the sketches and the bank letter in Gramps' office.

"Don't forget the map," Simon said.

I showed Marnie the map, the highlighted line leading to Paradise, and the words *Shipment #35 – GOLD* at the end.

Marnie leaned closer to check it out. "What's this?" She pointed to *Mildred must not know.*

"I think Gramps wanted to keep it a secret from Gram," I said. "I'm not sure why." While Simon picked up his scattered belongings, I filled in the details—the Alzheimer's that affected Gramps' brain, his strange behavior, his last day. "I'm pretty sure he was coming here."

"Shipment #35. No kidding," Marnie said.

"You've heard of it?" I asked.

Marnie fiddled with the *Stop the Flooding* button pinned to her t-shirt and stared at the lake in the distance. I followed her gaze. The water shimmered smooth as glass, empty except for one figure in the middle. Fortier. Paddling his canoe, looking very much alive despite the accident.

My despair returned. We were no closer to finding the gold. With time running out, what if Fortier was a step ahead of us?

CHAPTER 28

Simon adjusted his reassembled supply belt. "What are we going to do?"

I really didn't know what to say, but it dawned on me that Marnie hadn't answered all of my questions. "Why did you come here today? I asked again.

"Look around. See all this?"Marnie swept her arm over the landscape. She motioned to the concrete piles jutting out of the ground. "In the 40s, during World War II, this was a German prisoner of war camp. They dismantled the camp when the war ended and carted most of it away in pieces. All except these concrete piles. They were too deep and heavy to move."

"A German prisoner of war camp?" Simon said. "Here?"

"It's a forgotten piece of local history," Marnie explained. "Most people don't know about the camp and it's about to disappear."

She walked to the largest of the concrete piles. "See the lake? Pretty isn't it? Well, Hydro is planning to build a dam downstream. When it's finished, this whole area will be flooded. Lots of people are opposed to it." Marnie pointed to her button. "I'm one of them."

Marnie still hadn't answered my question, so I asked again. "So you came here because...?"

"When I saw you with the photos at the coffee shop, I thought you might know something about the camp."

"I don't get it," Simon said.

"Me either," I said.

"I'm trying to stop the hydro-electric project. If I can prove there's something worth keeping here, then there's a chance contractors won't go ahead with the dam and they'll build it in another place where it will do less damage." She looked at the lake again. "Did you find anything?"

"No. Nothing really," I said.

Marnie gazed at the lake, silent for long seconds. "Well, I guess that's it then." She dusted off her jeans and walked toward the path to the road. Partway, she wheeled around and returned. "My shift at the coffee shop starts in half an hour. If you like, I can give you a lift back to town."

I looked at Simon. He looked at me. We both checked our watches. With an hour to go before the bus departed, it was an offer we couldn't refuse. We followed the path past the concrete piles to the rutted road where Marnie had parked. With each step, metal clanked against metal in my backpack.

"Wait a minute." I dug into my pack and handed the compass to Marnie. "We have this."

While Simon gave Marnie the lowdown about Northern Airways, I dug through the bag again. "And we found this near the lake." I passed the strange piece of metal to Marnie.

"Actually, I found it," Simon said proudly. "We think it's from the plane."

"Is this the kind of proof you need?" I asked.

"It might be. You said the plane went missing in the 40s. That's about the time Whitewater Camp operated. Maybe there's a connection. It's a start anyway."

We didn't talk much on our drive back to town. Marnie cranked the volume on the radio, flooding the car with heavy metal music. She gunned the engine like a race car driver, kicking up spirals of dust. I hung on as we veered around corners and shot over ruts.

"Hey, neat compass," Simon said from the back seat. "We're heading north. No, northwest. Okay, make that west."

I thought of Gramps again. He'd started me on this journey, a journey he couldn't finish. I felt like I'd failed him. I thought of Fortier too. How close was he to claiming the gold? And then there was Gram. Fortier was using her, I was pretty sure of that. I couldn't bear to see her hurt, not after all she'd experienced. First her father disappeared. Then she lost Gramps. And now after four months of mourning, she was just getting back on her feet again. A mishmash of other thoughts crowded my mind. Olivia. My parents. Even Buster made an appearance. I wondered about them all.

"Do your folks know you're here?" Marnie asked out of the blue.

"Maybe," I said.

"What about you, Simon?"

"Um."

Marnie tapped the steering wheel with her fingers. "Yeah, that's what I figured. They'll be worried, don't you think?"

"What are you going to do? Tell the RCMP?" I asked.

Marnie looked at me, surprised. "No." Then she smiled. "Not just yet anyway."

"The officers in the coffee shop yesterday...were they looking for us?"

Marnie laughed. "My, aren't you the paranoid one? No, they were from the Minnedosa detachment, stopping for a bite to eat. Even cops need food, you know."

Marnie looked sixteen but acted older. "So what's the scoop?" I pointed to the tattoo on her arm with the name "Timmy" blazing across the center. "That your boyfriend?"

She didn't answer.

"I like it," Simon chimed. "It looks stupendous."

"Thanks, Simon. It's my favourite one."

Stones pinged the underside of the car as we rounded a wicked curve. "You would have liked Timmy," Marnie said more to herself than to us.

"Timmy?" I asked.

Marnie seemed surprised that I'd heard. "My younger brother. He died in a boating accident at Whitewater Lake four years ago." Then she told us about all about him. How Timmy had been her only brother. How the two of them had been close. How Whitewater Lake brought a rush of memories every time she visited.

We bumped along the final stretch of road. The teetering lumber mill with peeling paint greeted us as we entered the sad town of sagging buildings. Marnie screeched to a stop in front of the coffee shop and flung open the door.

"End of the road. It was a pleasure meeting both of you, but I've got to work now. If you like, you can wait inside till your bus comes."

Simon and I tumbled out of the car, back in Paradise. A dilapidated town with one road in, one road out and a single bus running each day, no further ahead that when we started.

"Now what?" Simon asked.

I didn't answer. I couldn't. I really didn't know what to say.

CHAPTER 29

We waited outside, gazing at the godforsaken street. The pavement radiated heat, deserted except for a lone, chugging car. Sun reflected off windows, making it impossible to see without squinting. Sweat puddled off our foreheads. We melted like chocolate bars in a microwave oven.

"Maybe we should go inside," Simon said.

"Yeah. Maybe." Despite the day's disappointments, something Marnie said stuck with me. The plane went missing in the 1940s, about the same time Whitewater Camp was operational. Was there a connection?

The sun edged behind a cloud, ending a blaze of reflections across the street. Buildings appeared like shimmering mirages. One stood out from the others. Two storeys tall, elegant, built of stone instead of wood.

"Come on, Simon."

"Where are you going? The bus will be here in half-an-hour."

"We'll be back in time. Come on, hurry."

We ran to the stone building that served as town hall, library and museum. One step ahead of Simon, I bolted up the stairs, taking them two at a time.

The upstairs was divided into two sections—a tiny library on one side, a slightly larger museum on the other. Artifacts crammed the museum, some in glass cases, some tacked to the wall or stacked on the floor, many donated by town residents. Small note cards explained their history and importance. What a disorganized place!

We wandered the tight aisles. After a bit of searching, we discovered information about Whitewater Camp tucked in a dark corner, sandwiched between medical instruments and photographs of the town in the 1930s.

"Get a load of this." Simon explored the displays like he was on a sugar high, picking up one object after another. "Wonder what this does?"

"Can I help you find something?" a clear and inviting voice asked.

Simon spun around, almost dropping a long, wooden instrument with strange-looking cups at either end.

The voice belonged to a tiny woman—even shorter than Gram, but thicker. She tied her grey hair back with a blue bandana and wore a colourful dress splashed with figures of flowers and birds. Strings of multicoloured beads swayed from her neck.

She pointed to the instrument in Simon's hand. "Do you know what that is?"

"Not really," he said.

"A stethoscope. A very early one. You've probably seen a modern version of it when you visit the doctor."

"Cool." Simon pressed the cup against my chest and listened at the other end. "Yep, you're still alive, Nate."

The woman smiled and studied my face. "Don't I know you?"

I shuffled uncomfortably. I didn't know her. Why did she think she knew me?

"Oh, I'm sorry," she said at last. "For a moment, I thought I recognized you. But you're new to town, aren't you?"

I nodded, not knowing what to say.

"My name is Agnes. I'm the volunteer librarian and curator of our tiny museum. Can I help you?"

"No, thanks. I think we've found it," I said.

"Well, if you need anything, don't be afraid to ask." She turned to Simon and gently took the stethoscope out of his hand. "You're welcome to pick up things and try them out. Just be careful. Many of them are irreplaceable."

Agnes swished away, taking all color from the otherwise drab place.

A sign hung over a glass display case: *Whitewater POW Camp*. The case held a photo album and artifacts like tools and other everyday objects. While Simon studied them, I scanned articles and photographs on the bulletin board above.

Built in 1943, Whitewater Camp held more than 400 German POWs—prisoners of war—who had been captured during World War II. To provide firewood to heat Canadian homes during winter, the POW's worked as lumberjacks in the surrounding forest. In an aerial photograph of the camp that looked pretty close to the one I found in Gramps' desk, I counted fifteen buildings—six bunkhouses for the men, a cookhouse and dining hall, hospital, garage, workshop and several small service buildings. A powerhouse equipped with generators provided electricity.

At the bottom of one article, I found this:

> In October 1945, shortly after the war ended, a wrecking company from Winnipeg began to remove the buildings. Salvageable items were carted to Dauphin, a town sixty kilometres north of the camp. They were stored there and later auctioned by the government. When winter arrived earlier than expected, the work of tearing down the buildings became impossible to continue. It was finished the following year.

Simon nudged me and pointed to a tin cup in the display case. "Didn't your grandfather have one of those?"

"Looks pretty much the same. This one is better condition, though."

We searched through other things in the display case to see if they matched the ones in Gramps' box. Most were ordinary—tools, cutlery, plates. Other than the cup none looked similar.

Simon flipped through the photo album. One black-and-white photo caught my attention.

"Whoa, back up, Simon. There. That one."

The photo showed five prisoners huddled in a group, dressed in identical uniforms. A large dark circle covered the back of one man's shirt. A long stripe ran along the outer seam of his pants.

"Hey, just like the clothes in the boxes," Simon squeaked.

A jangle of beads sounded behind us. Agnes swished to our side. "Did you find what you wanted?" She eyed the photo album. "Are you interested in the old camp? Not many people know about it. Not much of the place remains."

"No kidding," Simon said. "Just lumps of concrete."

"So you've been there. Good thing you went now. In a few months, there won't be anything left." As she spoke, Agnes played with the beads around her neck, idly twisting them in circles. Her eyes glazed over, and for a moment she seemed lost in the memory of another time.

"Have you ever...." I began. "Have you ever heard of something called Shipment #35?"

Simon punched my arm. "Thought that was supposed to be a secret," he hissed.

Agnes snapped to attention. She leaned closer to study me. "Of course. That's why you look so familiar."

"Huh?"

"Hardly anyone remembers Shipment #35 or asks about it," she said. "The last person who did was an older gentleman. He looked very much like you."

Simon's jaw dropped. A tiny squeak bubbled to his lips. "Ah... um...."

"When was he here?" I asked.

"Let's see. Two summers ago. Last summer too, I think."

I pulled out the Paradise ad. "Around the time of the auction?"

"Yes, I believe so. I remember thinking I should close the museum and bid on a few things myself. But then he came in." Agnes paused and squinted at me. "And now you're here too, looking just like him and asking the same questions." She smiled. "Do you want me to show you what I showed him the first time he came?"

Without another word, Agnes led us across the floor to the library side. She opened a tall filing cabinet, pulled out a thick folder and motioned to two wooden chairs. "Take your time." Then she pattered off, leaving us alone.

The folder contained newspaper clippings and photographs, loosely organized in chronological order. "Here." I gave Simon a few of the more recent ones from the bottom of the pile.

"What am I supposed to be looking for?"

"Anything about the plane or Shipment #35."

I started with the top page, an article from a newspaper dated November 22, 1945. *Gold Shipment Disappears.*

Below, in smaller print, a second headline read *Pilot and Engineer Missing.* Photographs of the plane and missing aviators lined the bottom of the page. I leaned in for a closer look and grabbed Simon's arm.

"What's up?"

A strangely familiar face stared back at me from the newspaper, a face I'd seen a few days ago in Gram's garage. Eyes like Gram's, nose like Mom's. There was no mistaking the family resemblance.

CHAPTER 30

Simon looked over my shoulder. "Those the guys on the plane?"

I nodded and pointed to one photograph. "I know that man."

Simon shrugged. "How could you? That picture is older than dirt."

Words caught in my throat. It was hard to explain. "That's Tom Hendricks."

"Who?"

"My great-grandfather. Gram's father."

Tom Hendricks wore a uniform like the kind used by officers during World War II. A cap, tilted to one side, covered his head. A wave of dark hair spilled from underneath.

Simon grabbed the article out of my hand. "How come you never told me about him?"

"I don't know much. It's a long story." I did the best I could to explain to Simon how Tom Hendricks abandoned his family, how Gram never talked about him, how he was a family secret.

"What a low life," Simon muttered, shaking his head.

We read the rest of the article together. The missing plane, a Bellanca Aircruiser, had been the largest plane in a fleet belonging to Northern Airways. On the way to Winnipeg from The Pas, a mining town in northern Manitoba, the plane and its shipment of gold coins disappeared. Radio contact was lost somewhere near Paradise, far south of the route normally used by planes travelling that way.

Simon sat on the edge of his chair, a knot of wrinkles across his forehead. "Maybe he died in the accident, only nobody knew for sure because the plane was never found."

"Maybe." But the more I thought about it, the less it made sense. "Why keep it a secret all these years? It's not like he left his family on purpose."

We thumbed through other articles and shared updates with one another. After the plane disappeared, a search and rescue effort failed to locate it, the shipment or the two men. One newspaper clipping, written two weeks after the incident, mentioned that the Bank of Montreal had posted a reward for information leading to the recovery of the missing coins.

"Hey," Simon waved an article in my face. "You got to read this."

I followed his finger as he traced every word. *Rumours persist that the gold shipment may not have been lost at all, but may have been stolen in a carefully orchestrated heist.*

Simon looked up. "What's a heist?"

"A carefully planned robbery."

'Oh," Simon's eyebrows shot up. "Oh, I get it now."

My grandmother's words came back to me. *He was a scoundrel. He abandoned his wife and children, left them high and dry at a time when they needed him most.* Was this the family secret? That Tom Hendricks had been a thief? That he'd ditched his family for a shipment of gold coins?

I flipped back to the first article, to the photograph of Tom Hendricks. Beside it was a second photograph—the pilot, a balding man in his forties named Mike Palmer.

"Wait a minute." Why did his name ring a bell? "Mike Palmer. MP. Those were the initials on the briefcase!"

"Really? Let's see." Simon grabbed the article. "Now that's interesting."

A shadow fell across the page and Simon grew quiet. "She's back," he whispered, nudging me.

Agnes leaned against the filing cabinet, studying us. "Have you found what you wanted?"

"I think so."

She pointed to the articles at our feet. "I was just a young girl then, but I remember it well. The plane vanished right after the war and the whole town buzzed with the news. A plane disappearing near Paradise, carrying a shipment of gold coins. Life in a small town doesn't get much more exciting than that. Most of the men in the search party came from Paradise."

Simon squirmed in the chair. "Did they ever find anything?" he blurted.

"Not a trace. They searched for days, right through one of the worst winter storms ever. It grew so cold they were forced to quit. It's doubtful anyone could have survived such horrible conditions."

Agnes gazed at the pictures. "They never did find the plane. Or those two men. That's when the rumours started. Folks couldn't figure out how a plane and two men could just disappear like that. Stories circulated that the plane hadn't crashed at all, that the men had flown south taking the shipment with them. To this day, some people in town still believe those two men assumed new identities elsewhere, and lived lives of luxury surrounded by piles of gold."

"Is that what you believe?" I asked.

"No. I don't. I don't believe the gentleman who was here before did either."

"He didn't?"

"No. I don't think he did. Do you mind telling me who he was?"

Simon jumped in before I could answer. "His grandfather. He came to find the gold, but he died a few months ago."

"Oh. I'm truly sorry," said Agnes.

I showed her the photograph. "Tom Hendricks was my great-grandfather. I'm not sure, but I think my grandfather came here to find him." I told Agnes about Gramps' confusion and his battle with Alzheimer's, the *Garden Supplies* box and the papers hidden in his desk. Her eyes widened when I mentioned the briefcase.

"Was it a brown leather briefcase with two handles? Old looking, torn in places?"

"Yes. Yes, it was," Simon said. "How did you know?"

Agnes smiled at Simon then turned back to me. "Your grandfather had it here last year. He may have gotten it at the auction. I can't be sure, but I recall thinking it was odd the way he clutched it. The briefcase looked so battered, but your grandfather treated it like a sacred object."

Suddenly the air felt heavy and stifling. Agnes examined me closely. "He was very protective of that briefcase. When his friend offered to carry it for him, he refused and became angry. It was all very strange."

"His friend?"

"The man who accompanied him last year. Shorter fellow, a bit unkempt. About your grandfather's age, I'm guessing. The two came together."

I struggled to breathe the hot soupy air.

Simon, meanwhile, had no problem speaking. "Why the dirty, no good, rotten...."

CHAPTER 31

My head ached. My mouth felt papery dry. The room swirled. I gripped the sides of the chair to keep from toppling over.

"Are you all right?" Agnes asked. "You're awfully pale."

"You look like you're going to puke," Simon said. He turned to Agnes and lowered his voice. "He's got a real weak stomach, you know."

"I heard that," I croaked. "I'm okay, really."

Agnes studied my face. "You sure?"

I focused on the floor to control my reeling stomach. Was it Fortier? "The man who was with my grandfather...did he walk with a limp and carry a cane?"

Agnes looked up at the ceiling, remembering. "Come to think of it, yes he did. It was a bit strange. They argued over the briefcase. But then there was a book too. They couldn't seem to agree what to do about that either."

"A book?"

Voices rose in the museum, interrupting our conversation. "Oh, dear," Agnes said. "I really must go. Are you sure you're okay?"

"Fine. Just fine."

Agnes padded away, leaving us alone. I sat too numb to move. Fortier. Here last year with Gramps.

"Farter was here," Simon said, echoing my thoughts. "Why the...."

I opened my backpack and took out the black book. Under the florescent lights I caught a glimmer, a reflected glow coming from the lower right corner.

"Look, Simon."

I hadn't noticed it before, but two letters were stamped on the cover. A set of initials. MP. I almost dropped the book. "The same initials on the briefcase. MP. Mike Palmer. The pilot."

Simon grabbed the book. "Really?"

He flipped through the pages, back to front, and frowned. "There's nothing. They're all blank. I don't get it."

I guided Simon to the window. "The light's better here."

We rummaged through pages, angling them to catch the light. Most of them looked blank, but others bore faint marks—words too faded to read.

"See that, Simon. There is something on these pages."

He zeroed in for a closer look. "I guess, but it would have to be a lot darker to actually read it."

His head jerked up, his mouth hung open. "Now wait a minute." He looked around the library. His eyes settled on a coin-operated photo-copier near the doorway. Like the old machine in Simon's room, this was an antique, dust-covered and without fancy buttons.

We scrounged through our pockets, hauled out coins and popped a few down the chute. The photocopier stuttered and whirred.

"Come on, baby." Simon hugged the machine, coaxing it to life.

I opened the book to a random page, placed it on the scanner and pressed the start button. The machine clattered and slowly spit out a glossy looking sheet.

"Hmmm…not much better."

Simon adjusted contrast and light settings then dropped a few more coins into the machine. On the second copy, the squiggles looked darker, but so did the background.

"Let's try this." Simon twisted a knob and punched a few buttons.

The next copy came out with fuzzy black letters against a splotchy grey background.

"Let's see." I angled the page. There were gaps, missing letters and words, but I could make out some of it: *Poor Mike is dead. He never had a chance.*

CHAPTER 32

We photocopied pages until we ran of coins.

Agnes shuffled over. "You've been busy." She glanced at the pages. "Not that I want to spoil your fun, but we'll be closing in a few minutes."

"You're closing?" I checked my watch. "The bus!"

Simon stood like a statue, his face drained of colour.

"Come on." I grabbed the photocopies with one hand, and pushed Simon to the exit with the other. I bolted down the stairs, two at a time, dragging Simon. He acted like a zombie, stiff as cardboard with his eyes locked in a vacant trance.

"Snap out of it, Simon," I yelled, yanking him harder.

We spilled into the street in such a rush that we almost slammed into the RCMP cruiser parked in front of the coffee shop. The echo of grinding gears rattled toward us from the gas station down the street. An engine roared and tires hummed against pavement. We stood paralyzed and watched as the bus tail lights grew smaller and smaller.

My shoulders sagged. My knees trembled. I dropped the photocopied sheets and watched numbly as they drifted to the pavement. We'd missed the only bus. How would we get back? And after popping coins down the photocopier, we were pretty much out of money too. Crashing failures. That's what we were.

"We missed it," Simon wailed.

"Yeah, I know."

"My dad is going to kill me. My life is over."

"Really?" I'd never seen Simon's dad get mad. Not ever. But my dad? Now that was a different story. "What's your dad going to do?" I asked.

Simon wiped away a tear. "Well, he'll take away my Game Boy."

"That's it?" I snorted. "That's nothing. I'm facing a prison sentence— a month of early curfews, minimum. And that's after my dad screams at me."

Simon kicked the dust. "He'll take away my cell phone too."

"Really? I'll lose my computer, my cell phone, and I'll probably have to cut the grass every day for the rest of the summer. Try topping that!"

Simon mulled this over. "Well…my dad will take away my TV." Then he whipped around and stabbed my chest with his finger. "No! He'll send me to the sitters. That's what he'll do. Oh, I am so dead, Nate. He's gonna kill me."

I stared at Simon and shook my head. Death by babysitter. Really?

Simon paced back and forth while I gazed down the street and re-hashed our options. What now?

"Oh, no!" Simon pointed to the coffee shop.

I wheeled around. Through a coffee shop window, I saw two officers talking to Marnie, the same two as the day before. One jotted in a small notepad. Marnie looked agitated. She gestured with her hands and pointed to the stone building behind us. The officers turned to look.

I pulled Simon behind the cruiser. Blood drained from his face. "Whad-a-we gonna do?" He waved a wad of photocopied pages in my face. "We missed the bus. My dad is going to kill me."

I thought of my own situation. My parents returning. Gram expect-ing me home soon. Olivia about to deliver the envelope. If Simon thought he was in trouble, it was nothing like the trouble I'd be in. I peeked at Marnie and the officers again. Still talking. Still taking notes. "What if you came home with a heap of gold, Simon? Think your dad would still be mad at you?"

Simon stopped fidgeting. He looked at the sweaty clump of pages in my hand. "Maybe not so much."

We spread the photocopies on the pavement and arranged them in order. We studied each page, trying to decode them, but between the faint writing and the gaps, some were indecipherable. A few pages seemed to be missing altogether. We had a giant puzzle in front of us.

The first half of the book listed compass readings, notes about times and locations, details about shipments—the gold coins of Shipment #35 among them—all written with a precise hand.

"Mike Palmer's flight log," Simon said. "He was the pilot, right?"

Midway through the flight log, the handwriting changed—wider loops, steeper slant, more spelling mistakes. Another person's handwriting. It had to belong to the only other person on the plane—Tom Hendricks, my great-grandfather.

"Listen to this," I read the words aloud. "Poor Mike is dead. He never had a chance…storm…pushed off course."

"Mike is dead," Simon whispered.

I smoothed out the crumpled page and read on. "Tried freeing Mike…crawled with Mike's bag…."

"He took Mike Palmer's briefcase!" Simon squeaked.

"Shh. Not so loud."

Fortunately the sleepy street was deserted, no cars, no pedestrians. I stole another look through the café window. The two officers were seated in a booth now, glasses of water already on the table. I continued reading out loud. "Found camp…took shelter…." I put the page down. "He crawled to the Whitewater camp. That's where he went after the plane crashed. Do you get what this means?"

"The gold is there?"

"Maybe." I scanned the page again, looking for fresh clues. "The rest is hard to read."

Somewhere down the street an engine backfired.

Simon shot to his feet. He glanced around and chewed his nails. "Whad-a-we gonna do? We can't just stay here."

Before I could answer, a voice interrupted, soft and lilting, yet stern too. "Just what are you two doing here?"

CHAPTER 33

Marnie crossed her arms. "You were supposed to be on the bus. What happened?"

"We missed it," said Simon.

I put my hands on my hips and pointed to the RCMP officers in the window. "What were you doing? Giving us up to the cops?"

Marnie lifted one eyebrow and laughed. "Oh dude. You do have quite the imagination. I wasn't telling them about you. I was telling them about the bear. Wildlife officials have been tracking the movements of bears through the area—part of the environmental assessment they're doing to study the impact of the hydro-electric project. I was telling the RCMP what I knew so they could pass the information along. That's all."

"Oh." I looked away, my face burning. "Oh, I see."

"Why did you guys miss the bus?" Marnie asked again. "Where were you anyway?"

Simon pointed to the museum.

Marnie's green eyes flashed. Her ruby red smile returned. She looked at the papers in my hand. "So what did you find?"

I noticed a new button on Marnie's shirt, a companion to *Stop the Flooding*. This one said *Act Now*.

"Go ahead," Simon said. "Show her."

I passed Marnie the photocopied pages and gave her a quick rundown. Her eyes lit up when I told her about Tom Hendricks and his connection to Shipment #35 and the Whitewater camp.

"Now that's something I might be able to use." she said. She thrust the pages back into my hands and we followed as she hurried across the street to the coffee shop. At the door, she stopped and turned.

"Wait here. Don't move a muscle."

"What was that all about?" asked Simon.

I shrugged. "Who knows?"

In minutes, Marnie returned, a jacket under her arms, a flashlight in her hand. She ushered us to her car. "Let's go."

"Where?" I asked.

Simon scrambled into the back seat. "You're driving us home?"

"Not exactly."

"I thought you had to work," I said.

"Don't worry. I took care of that."

We ripped down the main drag and veered around the lumber mill. Marnie jacked up the radio, blasting rock from all four speakers. Simon bobbed with the music and mouthed the words. I stared ahead and stole glances at Marnie's tattoos. Vines looped up her arms, weaving intricate patterns of leaves and flowers. Where the vines met the heart, they crisscrossed and burst into colourful hands.

"You miss him?" I said.

Marnie glanced at me, then at her arm. "Timmy? Yes, I do. Some days I feel that he's right beside me."

Like Gramps. I could feel his presence even in this far-off place.

Marnie focused on the rutted road that dipped and twisted through stands of pines and aspens, the same road Gramps travelled last summer and the summer before, the road leading to Whitewater Camp. To where Tom Hendricks took refuge after the crash. To where we'd find the downed plane. The gold too. I was sure of it.

By the time we reached the trailhead, the sun had edged past the trees. Far off clouds billowed like distant sailing ships heading our way. We poured out of the car, grabbed our gear, and wound down the trail past pines and thick grasses. Simon swung his sword as he led the way.

When we entered the clearing, Marnie stopped at the largest concrete pile. She gazed across to Whitewater Lake, rippling like a silver jewel before us. "All this is going to disappear," she said. "I can't let that happen." Her fingers wrapped around her arm and Timmy's heart. "I just can't."

To the left of the lake, smoke curled above towering trees. Simon elbowed me. "Farter," he mouthed behind Marnie's back. "He's still here."

"Can you read those pages again?" Marnie said.

Simon huddled over the pages and followed my finger as I traced

out the words. "Poor Mike is dead. He never had a chance…storm…
pushed off course…tried freeing Mike…crawled with Mike's bag…
found camp."

"That's all?"

"Other than a word here or there that doesn't make sense, yes, that's it."

Marnie pondered the lake. "We might have missed something. Simon, can you show me where you found that piece of metal? Maybe we'll find more there."

Simon led her across the clearing, yapping excitedly. "Imagine. Piles of gold. We'll be rich. Filthy rich!"

"Are you coming, Nate?" Marnie called over her shoulder.

A cool gust blew through the woods, rustling the pages and nearly tearing them from my hands. I clenched them tighter and turned away from the stiff breeze.

"I'll look around here," I yelled back.

The strange wind. Here again.

I tore through my backpack. Had I missed something? The sketch of the concrete pile caught my attention. It matched the view before me, but unlike the light and airy look of the real thing, the drawing was filled with heavy shadows and depressing shades. The work of Alzheimer's, I assumed. But now I noticed something else. Proportions in the sketch were skewed. Objects in the foreground—the concrete pile, the grasses around it, the logs nearby—looked smaller than they did in real life. Things in the background, though, appeared unrealistically large.

Gramps used different styles to draw the two. Narrow lines and light shades for the foreground. Wide lines and heavy shades for the background. The effect was eerie. I stared into the distance, past thickets of berries, past immense trees to the lake. And then I looked at the sketch again. The background seemed to jump right out of the page.

The lake. The background was the lake, looming larger than life, darker and bolder. Did Gramps want it to be noticed?

While Simon and Marnie investigated the lake shore, I dug out other sketches and wandered to the places where Gramps stood to draw them. To the rotten log. In its sketch, the lake overshadowed the foreground. At the gnarled tree beside the creek. The lake again. The lake, always more dark and dramatic than real life. The only object repeated in all three sketches.

What did it mean?

CHAPTER 34

By the time I reached Marnie and Simon, I was so out of breath my words sounded like they'd been mixed in a blender.

"Fa-sum-tin," I said, panting.

"What?" said Simon. "Slow down, will ya?"

"I…found…something." I led them to the concrete pile and pointed to the sketch. "See. There's the lake, big as Texas in the background. The other sketches are like that too."

"Oh, I see," Simon said, but I could tell from his dazed look that he really didn't.

Marnie, though, caught on right away. "Nate's grandfather may have exaggerated the background."

"Oh, I see," Simon said again, nodding like a bobble head. Then he stopped, shrugged and turned to Marnie. "Did we find the gold or not?"

Marnie led Simon to a fallen log and sat beside him. "Nate's grandfather might have been trying to send a message when he drew these. But we don't know his state of mind. Was he thinking clearly or was he confused? Alzheimer's does weird things to people."

"But I thought for sure these were clues," I said.

"Sorry, Nate. You were really hoping for more, but…you sure there's nothing else in the flight log?"

By now the photocopied pages were a gummy wad. I unpeeled the papers, smoothed out wrinkles, and searched through the scattered words. "It says…crawled with Mike's bag…found camp…took shelter…."

"Yeah, we heard that before," said Simon.

"But there's something else on the next page. See plane…used to be…."

Marnie's eyes narrowed. "See plane...used to be...."

"I don't get it." Simon said.

The choir of wolves broke into a chorus again. Their howls ricocheted across the clearing, signalling the approach of twilight. A pink hue bled across the sky and the moon rose in the distance. Evening cool replaced daytime heat.

Twilight? So soon?

I checked my watch. Nearly eight-thirty. In a half hour or so, the bus from Paradise would pull into Winnipeg, two persons short of its intended cargo. I imagined the scene that followed when we didn't show up at home when promised. Olivia delivering the note. Gram overcome with worry. My parents furious. Mr. Sloan wondering if he could ever trust Simon again. Would they call the cops? Start a search, hoping against hope their kids were safe?

No point in panicking. Nothing I could do anyway. So I thought about where I stood—in the footsteps of men long dead. Time collapsed. An eerie calm came over me. Snippets of my dream returned. Men in this same forest carrying axes. Gramps leading the crew. Another man, holding something, joining him.

Who was the man? Where were they headed?

I closed my eyes and played the dream again. The men wore uniforms. Red circle on the back of their shirts. Red stripes running down the pant legs. I looked past the German prisoners to the man beside Gramps. Shorter and slimmer than him.

Tom Hendricks, my great-grandfather. The guy in the newspaper clippings was the man walking beside Gramps.

I squeezed my eyes tighter and watched the men stroll through a familiar clearing, past thickets ripe with berries, past soaring pine trees, to the edge of the shimmering lake. Gramps and Tom Hendricks stopped, turned, and waved to me.

Images of the lake snapped me back to reality. I pulled out Gramps' sketches and spread them on the ground, a jigsaw of puzzle pieces that seemed to highlight the body of water. "Gramps wanted us to notice the lake," I said. "We know Tom Hendricks crawled to the camp. What happened after he got here?"

Simon read from the photocopied pages. "Found camp, took shelter."

Marnie jumped in. "See plane, used to be."

"But what does that mean?" Simon asked.

Marnie grinned. "He could see the plane from camp. From his shelter. But maybe the plane wasn't where it used to be. It had disappeared."

"Right!" I gathered the sheets and sketches. "The plane crashed on the ice of Whitewater Lake, but then it sank and disappeared."

"I get it." Simon said, finally catching on. "Tom Hendricks could see the lake."

Simon slapped Marnie on the back, then shrank back when he realized what he had done. His face turned grey. "Wha...ah...um...."

Marnie punched Simon's arm and laughed. "You're pretty smart, kid."

I took out the aerial photograph of the camp. Simon and Marnie crowded around, trying to catch a glimpse under the flashlight's narrow beam. The buildings of Whitewater Camp radiated around a circle with the mess hall at the centre. On the far left of the photo stood Whitewater Lake. Between the lake and the buildings, tall pines rimmed the clearing. "Look. There's only one building at the camp with a clear view of the lake." With my finger, I traced a straight line from the lake through an opening in the trees to the camp. "There."

"The powerhouse," Marnie said.

"The powerhouse," Simon echoed.

We ran across the field to the spot where the powerhouse once stood. In celebration, we danced in a circle under the soft glow of the moon.

"We found it. We found it." Simon chanted. He grabbed Marnie's arm and they twirled around. He reached to grab my arm too, but stopped. "What did we find?"

Marnie and I stopped too. We looked at each other. What had we found? What were we celebrating anyway? Tom Hendricks had taken shelter at the powerhouse in the winter of 1945, after the camp had been abandoned, but before it had been completely taken down. So what? We still didn't know what happened to him or what became of the gold.

Simon checked his watch. In the growing dark, his face looked white as bleached cotton. "Nine o'clock," he gulped. "The bus just arrived in Winnipeg. I am so dead. Whad-a-we gonna do?"

CHAPTER 35

Simon recovered before I did. While I mentally ran through the options, he jabbed the keypad of his phone and paced nervously. "I'm not getting a signal. Anyone else?"

I tried mine. "Nope."

"No, not working for me either," Marnie said. "We're probably too far from a tower."

I tried to console Simon. "I left a note with Olivia that she's supposed to pass on to Gram if we don't show up on time. It explains everything."

Simon looked at me like I'd lost my mind. "Really? That's going to keep us out of trouble? I am so dead."

I ran my fingers through my hair, and patted down the stubborn patch. I imagined the reaction at home. Gram worrying. Mom fretting. Dad fuming, his cloud of anger building. I could almost hear his voice: "That kid. Nothing but trouble." My summer would be ruined. Extra chores. No friends over. Hunkered down in my room for the next month.

"When we get back to town, you can use a land line to call home. I can drive you now, if you like," Marnie offered.

"But we still don't know what happened to Tom Hendricks or if he took off with the gold," I said. I'd failed Gramps. I just couldn't go back empty-handed.

Marnie sat on the concrete pile, gazing at the lake. "We actually know quite a lot. The plane is submerged in the lake, and there's a historical connection to this place. It's probably enough to put the hydro-electric project on hold for a while."

Simon stopped pacing, tore open his backpack and tossed out objects. A shovel landed in a berry bush. A metal plate clanged off a concrete pile. A t-shirt latched on a branch like a Christmas ornament.

"What are you doing?" I asked.

Simon held up a lantern, twice the size of his flashlight and three times as bright as Marnie's. "Since we're stuck here anyway, we might as well take this investigation to the next level." He wedged the lantern between two rocks and aimed it at the place where the powerhouse once stood. He walked across the tall grass, waved his flashlight and crouched down with the magnifying glass for a closer look.

What was he up to? Marnie and I followed Simon.

"What are we looking for?"

"The past."

"I don't get it. What do you mean?"

Simon waved the flashlight around. He spoke slowly, like an impatient teacher dealing with a difficult student. "Even though the powerhouse is gone, there are still probably signs of its existence here." He shone the light at a slab of concrete barely visible in the tall grass. "See that. Probably the original foundation. And that," he shifted the light to a patch of grass much taller than the rest, "that could be where something organic is buried."

"Organic?"

"Stuff that decays. Food, garbage—"

"A dead body?" I asked.

"Maybe."

"Where'd you learn all this?" asked Marnie.

Simon put his hands on his hips and puffed out his chest. "The Internet."

We continued to search for clues. Not far from the foundation, I stumbled over a shallow depression in the ground about the size of manhole cover.

"Simon, shine the light here. What's this? Anything important?"

Simon nodded. "Maybe.

Marnie and I huddled over the dip in the soil while Simon ran for his backpack. He fished out a few items. A broom handle about a metre long. A battery-operated radio, the size of a small box of candy. Two rings cut out of plywood, one the size of a dinner plate, the other the size of a saucer, both covered with ten to fifteen coils of copper wire. The smaller ring was set inside the larger one and held in place with narrow strips of wood.

"Okay," I said, "Now I've seen everything. What are you going to pull out next? A rabbit?"

In quick order, Simon assembled the pieces, securing the plywood rings with duct tape near one end of the broom handle and the radio near the other. He connected the two with a strand of wire.

"Looks like some voodoo apparatus," I said. "What's it supposed to do? Communicate with the dead?"

Simon stared at me, clearly disgusted. "It's a metal detector. Can't you tell?"

Marnie ruffled Simon's hair. "Oh, Simon. You're so smart."

Simon turned on the radio and cranked up the volume. Static hissed from the speaker.

"Nothing but interference," I said. "It's not working."

"Watch and learn, Nate."

Simon waved the contraption over the ground, keeping the plywood discs a few centimeters above the surface. Static crackled in spurts and pops, louder in some places, softer in others. When he hit the dip in the ground, the device spewed a faint but steady stream of static.

"There." Simon pointed to a patch of weeds in the center of the sunken area.

While I held the flashlight, Marnie grabbed the shovel and dug. About ten centimeters below the surface, the shovel clanged against something solid. Marnie tossed the shovel aside, dug with her fingers and pulled out a pencil-shaped object, thick as my finger.

"A metal spike?' I said. "Really? Is that all there is?"

"Patience, Nate." Simon adjusted the plywood rings, moving them closer to the end of the broom handle and then fired up the volume on the radio. "That should increase its sensitivity. Let's try again."

Swishing the detector back and forth, Simon walked the same area again. Not more than a metre in, the detector screeched. Marnie dug. This time, she pulled a brass button from the soil. Simon shrugged. "Well, it's something."

With each pass of the metal detector, we discovered other objects—a wrench, half a dozen tacks, three pennies, a coil of copper wire, and buried deepest of all—an iron rod thicker than my arm and half its length.

Simon stuffed the lighter items into his backpack. "Like I always say—"

"Never hurts to be prepared," I blurted. "Right, got it."

The flashlight in my hand flickered and dimmed. I checked my watch. "We've been at this an hour." Another hour gone. For what? Guilt balled up into a fist and sucker punched me in the gut. Gram. My parents. Mr. Sloan.

"A few more minutes," Simon said. "We're getting close. I can feel it."

On the next pass, the radio screeched its loudest ever. "Jackpot," Simon shouted.

Marnie shoveled around the edges of a rectangular object. Simon dragged the lantern and positioned it over the hole while I scraped away the last bit of dirt with my fingers. "It's some kind of metal box."

Embossed vines scrolled across the lid and sides of a container roughly the size of a box of chocolates. I fished out the box and shook it. Something rattled and clinked inside.

"It looks too small to hold a shipment of gold. Definitely not heavy enough either. What do you suppose is in it?"

I tried prying it open, but years of corrosion sealed the lid.

"Let me have a go." Simon grabbed a rock and hammered the lip.

"What, no hammer in the bag?" I teased. "You brought along everything else."

Simon grinned and kept hammering. "It...It's coming."

Between the clang of rock hitting metal, other sounds caught my attention. Twigs breaking. Branches swishing. The movement of something large getting closer.

Simon must've heard it too because he froze in mid strike. "It's a bear!" He tossed aside the rock and dropped the box. "Run."

He bolted into the forest.

Marnie ran after him, shouting, "Stop! Don't run!"

I hesitated and then ran after them too. A few paces away, I remembered the box and veered back to scoop it up. As I tucked the box under my arm, a shadow broke through the trees. I ran away from it, through the clearing, past the berry patch, my feet clipping stones and weeds. Ahead, Whitewater Lake shimmered in the moon-glow, the missing plane deep below its waters. Mike Palmer was inside. Maybe the gold too.

I glanced over my shoulder and my foot snagged a vine. I tripped. Instinctively, I held out my hands to break my fall. The box flew into the dark ahead. I careened to the side. On the way down, I cracked my skull on a rock.

Lights out.

CHAPTER 36

When I came to, it was dark as pitch, except for the moon which was a glowing orb above me. My head ached like it had been split by an axe. I reached up to check the damage and touched a strip of cloth wrapped around my head like a turban.

"Good. You're awake," a gravelly voice said.

I pushed up on my elbows. Fortier sat beside a campfire along the lakeshore, stick in hand, stirring the flames. Embers swirled like fireflies into the night sky. Smokey wisps circled above his head.

I sat up the rest of the way. "Whaaa…" Too fast, I guess. My stomach churned; my head swooned. "I think I'm going to be sick." My scrambled brain connected the dots. Running…tripping…falling.…"Ah, how did I get here?"

Fortier prodded a log, creating a shower of sparks. Stubble covered his chin. His clothes were rumpled. Under the glow of the fire, his face looked mottled—like white glue mixed with orange paint had been dabbed on his skin. "So you figured it out, did you?" he said.

I played dumb. "Figured what out?"

Slowly, the fog in my head cleared. Simon? Marnie? Where were they? Where was the bear? And what happened to the box?

Fortier seemed to read my mind. "Your friends ditched you and headed for the road. You didn't. Not a smart move, was it?"

I didn't answer. Safer that way. I stood, fought a wave of dizziness and sat down again. Something clicked, though. "There wasn't any bear, was there? It was you prowling through the bush, wasn't it?"

Fortier smiled, teeth flashing orange in the firelight. "Seems you dropped this over there." He held up the metal box and motioned to a shrub behind him.

I lunged for the box, but my head ached. My legs felt like they'd sprouted springs. I managed only a few wobbly steps.

"Better rest," Fortier said. "Nasty head wound you have there."

I took his advice. I sat downwind from Fortier, a not too smart choice as it turned out. Clouds of smoke billowed my way. I coughed and gagged.

Fortier stirred the fire. Neither of us spoke.

Two lights wove through the forest, one three times brighter than the other. Distant voices called. "Nate! Nate! Where are you?"

"Over here," I croaked.

The lights grew closer, the voices louder. Fortier threw on another log and stirred the fire with the stick. Flames shot skyward. Embers exploded like rockets.

"Nate's here," he bellowed.

Two figures emerged from the darkness, one tall, arms riddled with tattoos, voice like a finely tuned harp. The other small and ghostly pale, hiding behind her.

Marnie ignored Fortier and rushed to me. "What happened?" She ran her fingers over my head and shone the flashlight in my face. "You look awful."

Simon hung back. He aimed the lantern at Fortier like it was some kind of death ray, opened his mouth then closed it again.

"What are you doing here?" Fortier grumbled. He reached up and touched the band aid that partly covered a huge purple welt on his forehead. "Up to no good, for sure."

Marnie swung around. "What's going on? Who are you?"

Fortier studied Marnie's tattoos. "What's your part in all this, missy? You bust into any garages lately, flatten any tires or hide an old man's license plates? How about…?" He reached over and pulled the black book from my back pocket. "How about stealing stuff like this? You a crook like them?"

Simon gasped. Before Marnie could say a word, Simon lunged out of the shadows and whipped a piece of paper out his pocket. He waved the wanted poster in Fortier's face. "You're the one with the criminal record, Farter."

Never had I seen Simon act so quickly or with such determination. It was as if he'd donned a superhero's cape. Beaming with pride, I gave Simon the thumbs up and a smile of encouragement.

"Yeah. You're the criminal," I said to Fortier.

Fortier gazed at Simon. A smile replaced his shocked look. He snatched the poster out of Simon's hands. "Well, what have we here? Proof of your break-in, I think."

Simon's jaw dropped. He stepped behind Marnie, ghostly white all over again.

Marnie eyed the poster, stared at Fortier, then turned to me. "What's going on, Nate? I think I deserve an explanation."

Fortier smiled smugly. "Yes, Nate. Explain your way out of this one."

I did my best. Fortier took it pretty well. He didn't interrupt as I painted a grey picture of his involvement—the way he'd been using Gram, sneaking through her house, prying her for information. I told Marnie about the *Garden Supplies* box that Fortier had stolen, his interest in my box, and the fishing trip he'd lied to Gram about taking.

"He came here last year with Gramps just as Gramps was getting worse. He used Gramps to get his hands on the gold, just like he's using Gram now." I snatched the wanted poster out of Fortier's hands. "He's a criminal."

"Is this true?" Marnie asked Fortier.

Fortier smiled. He shook his head and stoked the fire, shooting fresh embers into the sky. "I can see how this must look, but you've got it all wrong."

"Yeah, well enlighten us," I snapped. I threw a log on the fire, narrowly missing Fortier's head on purpose.

Fortier leaned to the side and dodged a shower of sparks. "I'm not who you think I am. Yes, I have a criminal past, robbed a bank or two in my day, but I paid my dues in prison. After that, I put my experience to good use. Firms pay me to test out their security systems, detect flaws and correct them. Banks and insurance companies hire me to recover stolen goods. I've been hunting for Shipment #35 for some time."

"So you used Gramps and Gram to get your hands on the gold. Nice play, Al-bert," I said.

"Not quite." Fortier kept his voice steady as he stirred the flames. "Your grandfather and I weren't close buddies—not at first, but eventually we warmed up to each other. Harold told me about Paradise and Tom Hendrick's disappearance. For Mildred's sake he wanted to find out what happened before it was too late. And yes, I wanted to find Shipment #35."

I jumped to my feet, fighting nausea, dizziness and an influx of smoke. "What a bunch of crap. Gramps hated you."

Fortier looked up. He didn't seem surprised by my outburst. "I imagine this is hard for you to believe, but here...." He reached into his pocket for a tattered piece of paper. "This fell out of the book when you ran off with it. Would you mind reading the line at the top?"

He passed the paper to me. A single sentence ran across the top. Forward scrawl, wide loops. *Albert, Mildred must not know.*

A chill swept through me. Marnie shivered. Simon's teeth chattered. Fortier pulled up the collar of his shirt.

"I don't get it," I said.

Fortier explained. How Gramps had travelled to Paradise by himself more than once. How he'd discovered things from the plane and Whitewater Camp at the annual auction. How he'd given a box of them to Fortier for safekeeping.

He winced and massaged his lame leg. "Bothersome thing. Arthritis and a stroke together. Not a good combination. Some days are worse than others. Now where was I?"

"Gramps. The gold."

"Ah, yes. By then Harold's memory was hazy and he was often confused. I don't think he trusted himself any longer. He swore me to secrecy. 'Mildred must not know,' he told me. He said it over and over as if repeating it would help him to remember."

I glanced at the torn page. Gramps must have been desperate to trust Fortier.

The old man rose, gripped his cane for support, breathing hard from the effort. "Harold figured that locating the gold would prove your great-grandfather didn't steal it. It would restore Tom Hendricks' reputation and give your grandmother some peace. But we hit a dead end."

All along, I assumed Fortier had been using Gram to get to the gold, and because Gramps once despised and distrusted him, I should feel the same way. Maybe I'd been wrong.

It wouldn't be the first time.

Fortier passed the book to me. "This was in the briefcase. Your grandfather and I never could figure out what was written in most of it." He glanced at the torn page in my hand. "Just that last page. Would you mind reading the bottom too?"

Below Gramps' scrawl other words crossed the page. They were faint, written in a different style by a different hand long ago. My great-grand-father's handwriting. I read it out loud. "Four days have passed since the crash…food gone…face a difficult decision…I must go."

"Tom Hendricks left? Where did he go?" asked Marnie.

"And did he take the gold with him?" I wondered aloud.

"Exactly my question," said Fortier.

A shower of sparks lit the sky as a fresh log hit the fire. We looked back. Simon stood in the orange glow, taller than I'd ever seen him, feet apart, chest out. Above his head, he held the metal box.

"Maybe the answer is in here," he said.

CHAPTER 37

While Simon and Marnie looked for another rock to hammer off the lid, I joined Fortier beside the fire. It wasn't easy to suddenly shift gears and trust someone I loathed only a short time ago. Without Gramps' note to Fortier, I doubt I would have shared anything.

I showed Fortier the photocopied pages and explained what we knew. The plane was at the bottom of Whitewater Lake. Mike Palmer's body was inside, a casualty of the doomed flight. Tom Hendricks survived the crash, took shelter at the powerhouse and fled four days later. It seemed like a tiny bit of information for all the risks we'd taken.

"How do you know the box contains anything remotely connected to Tom Hendricks?" Fortier asked.

"We don't, but we found it at the powerhouse so…." It was a long shot, but we'd been cruising on luck for some time already. Maybe it would hold a bit longer.

"I hope you're right," Fortier said, his voice a gravelly whisper. "Mildred is a very special lady. I would never want to see her hurt in any way."

The pages slipped from my hand. I jerked my head around, stealing a glance at Fortier. He nodded at me and smiled. Then he stood up, grunting from the effort. He teetered for moment and grabbed a nearby log.

"Harold brought us all here. Let's offer a toast to him." He tossed the log into the fire, unleashing an explosion of sparks. "Here's to your grandfather."

Fortier passed his stirring stick to me and winked. I smiled and jabbed the fire, coaxing another spray of sparks. "To Gramps." I said. Then I grabbed another log and tossed it on to the fire. "Here's to Gram too."

"To Mildred," Fortier echoed.

Gram! I checked my watch. We should have been home two hours ago. By now, everyone would know we're missing. Restless, I paced around the fire and pictured Gram's kitchen, everyone around the table. Gram fretting, waiting for my phone call. Mom holding back tears. Dad seething, watching the clock. Olivia drilling G.I. Joe, "Find Simon and Nate, will ya?" Buster? He'd be there too, curled at Olivia's feet, waiting just like the others.

And what about Simon's father? Would he be there too, pacing and wringing his hands with worry?

At last, Simon and Marnie returned. Simon lugged his backpack. He threw it on the ground, dug around, flinging objects aside

"What? No rock?" I said.

"Nope. Something better. Like I always say, it never—"

"—hurts to be prepared." I finished for him. "Yeah, I know."

Fortier stared at the growing pile at Simon's feet and shook his head. "People say I'm a packrat. You've got me beat, Simon."

Simon smiled, dug some more, then finally held up two objects—the axe in one hand, the metal spike he'd dug up earlier in the other.

"That should do it," he said, handing them to me.

I set the metal box on a large flat stone near the water's edge while Marnie held the lantern above it. "Do you want to join us?" I asked Fortier.

He smiled. "No. This is your time, Nate. It's what your grandfather would have wanted."

From the wild wind at the garage sale to this moment at Whitewater Lake, Gramps had led the way. Fortier was right. It would be what Gramps wanted.

Simon positioned himself above the box like a surgeon embarking on a delicate operation. "First, loosen the lid."

I tapped the edges of the lid a few times with the axe.

"Now use the spike as a lever," Simon commanded.

I wedged the spike under the lip and pushed. It took a few attempts but finally the lid popped off. I pulled out a disk the size of a large button, but heavier. Simon brought the lantern closer. "Well, what is it?"

"A coin. Canadian. Gold, I think. It looks new."

"Is there a date on it?" Marnie asked.

I squinted at the fine script. "1945."

Simon leaped up and danced for joy. He stopped when he noticed that no one else joined him. "What's it mean?"

Fortier piped up from his place beside the fire. "It doesn't mean much by itself. It's only one coin and there were thousands minted that year. It could have come from anywhere. Is there anything else, Nate?"

I pulled out a small sheet of paper, so delicate it almost fell to pieces when I unfolded it.

A soft breeze rustled the page.

"Hold the lantern steady. There's something written on it."

I recognized the handwriting immediately—same as in the second half of the flight log, nothing fancy, letters tall and sloped.

"You gonna read it or what?" Simon said.

> November 22, 1945
> I, Tom Hendricks, flight engineer, leave this note as my final record of events involving Northern Airways Flight 22. Should I not survive, perhaps my words will instead.
> Unfortunate circumstances brought down the plane. A wild winter storm came from nowhere, pushing us off course and we crashed on to the thin ice of a lake. The plane rapidly took on water and although I tried freeing the pilot, Mike Palmer, he was already dead and trapped in the crumpled cockpit. I narrowly escaped with just a few belongings, but was forced to leave Mike's body with our shipment.

I stopped reading and we looked to the lake. Deep beneath the water lay the plane, a decaying shell, long lost, but not quite forgotten. In the cockpit, the remains of Mike Palmer. In the hull, the gold coins of Shipment #35.

Gramps knew. Somehow he did. Now we had the proof we needed.

A gust of cool wind rustled the pages. Waves, barely ripples a moment ago, crashed against the shore. I shivered and tightened my grip as I read on.

> I found the remnants of a deserted camp and took shelter in the only building still standing. Now, the storm is over. What little food I had

*is now gone and I am relying on snow for mois-
ture. I doubt I will be found in time....*

The words were barely out of my mouth when the wind picked up,
spewing foamy waves at our feet. The temperature seemed to drop by
20 degrees.

"Oh my gosh," Marnie zipped up her jacket. "Hurry."

I clutched the page, shielding it from the wind as I read.

To my loving family, I think of you often....

Just then clouds streamed across the sky and hid the moon. Rain
splattered, a few drops at first, then a whole torrent.

"Run for it," Simon shouted, pulling his hoodie over his head.

Water splashed down Marnie's face. "Back to the car. Now!" She
grabbed my arm to pull me along.

"But there's more," I yelled.

"Never mind that. Hurry!"

I stuffed the paper back in the box, replaced the lid, pocketed the
coin and turned to run, but my legs wouldn't move.

Lightning flashed. The sky lit up like a thousand watt candle and
I saw ghostly images of Simon running across the clearing, Marnie
trailing after, and Fortier hobbling towards the path that led to his
campsite.

"Wait!"

Out of range now, Marnie and Simon kept running, but Fortier spun
around so quickly he almost lost his balance.

"Better get moving," he shouted.

"I can't."

Fortier limped back, grabbed my arm and pulled.

Legs like blocks of concrete. Feet nailed to the ground.

Gramps again.

Suddenly, I knew what I had to do. "I have a favour to ask," I hollered.

Fortier leaned in close, his ear to my mouth. I could barely hear myself over the howling wind, but he nodded as I spoke.

Then, just as quickly as it started, the storm died and the clouds part-
ed to reveal the moon again.

CHAPTER 38

After the hurricane wind at Whitewater Lake, our ride back to Paradise was uneventful. I expected Simon to be bubbling with excitement, but he nodded off in the back seat the moment Marnie turned the key.

Marnie sped off, shifting gears, spewing gravel. We said little—just a few words to recap what we knew.

"I think we have enough to halt the dam project," she said, rounding a sharp turn.

I slid into the door and hung on to the dashboard. "Probably."

"Was it worth it?" she asked.

"Worth it?"

"Running off, lying about it, dragging Simon along. Was it worth it?"

"Probably," I said. But maybe that was just another lie. We'd found the gold, the whereabouts of the plane, and the truth about Tom Hendricks, but weighed against the worry we caused and the trouble we were in, was it really worth it?

Marnie tore through town, past the coffee shop and down a side street. She screeched to stop outside a small, neat two storey house with colorful signs on the lawn. *Stop the Flooding. Preserve Our History. Together We Can Make a Difference.*

Simon stirred and yawned. "Where are we?" He stumbled out of the car and veered across the driveway.

With Marnie supporting Simon on one side and me on the other, we steered up the steps. Marnie's dad, a lumberjack-sized man, helped navigate Simon up the narrow stairs. When Simon hit Timmy's old bed, he clutched the pillow and moaned. "Oh, it's good to be home." Then he rolled over, lost in sleep once more.

Marnie's parents, Mr. and Mrs. Dohanski, listened to her explanation while I hovered speechless nearby. When Marnie mentioned our discoveries, her parents cheered.

"Oh, that is the best news ever, dear," said her mother.

Mr. Dohanski slapped me on the back with a meaty hand. "Wonderful. Just wonderful."

When Marnie explained my circumstances, Mrs. Dohanski threw her arms around me. "Of course, you boys can stay here tonight."

I doubt my parents would have responded like that. In fact, I know they wouldn't, but Marnie's parents were a different breed. They nodded, asked a few questions, and made only a few requests of me. "Phone your parents. Simon's father too. It's midnight. They must be very concerned."

Gram answered on the first ring.

"Nate?" I thought I heard a sniffle. "I've been waiting for your call. Are you okay? What about Simon?"

I pictured Gram in her kitchen, the phone beside her, my note spread on the table, my parents sitting nearby biting their nails. "I'm sorry, Gram. I didn't mean to worry you. We're both fine."

My father got on the line next. "What were you thinking, Nate? Taking off like that, dragging Simon along. And lying too? Where's your head anyway?"

"But—"

"Do you know the worry you caused here? I am so, so disappointed in you." I held the phone inches from my ear while Dad blasted on.

"But Dad—"

"I can't believe you could be that irresponsible, Nate."

"Dad, I can explain."

"I doubt it," he ranted. "Just wait until you get home. No TV. No computer—"

"Dad!" I shouted. "DAD! Can I say something?"

"It better be good," he said, calmer this time.

I pitched an offer and held my breath while Dad mulled it over.

"Okay, deal," he said. "But it better be good. And you have to get Mr. Sloan to agree too."

Just before the call ended, Dad said one more thing. "I'm really glad you're okay, Nate."

I almost dropped the phone. "Uh, thanks Dad."

Simon's father answered on the first ring. "Is Simon okay?"

"He's sound asleep."

That was true enough, but it took a bit of reassurance from Marnie's mother to really soothe Mr. Sloan's nerves.

"Not a scratch on him," she told Mr. Sloan. "Simon is fine here. It's no trouble, really."

"Mr. Sloan," I said, when I got back on the line, "I wonder if you could do something for—"

"That boy of mine. Always up to something. I really don't know what I'm going to do with him," he muttered. "What were you saying?"

"There's a box in Simon's room that I really need."

"A box? Simon's room is filled with boxes."

"This one's different. Size of a small microwave oven. *Garden Supplies* written on the top and sides."

He listened politely as I outlined my plan.

"Would you do that for me?" I asked.

"Sure," he said after a long pause. "No problem."

Mrs. Dohanski laid a sleeping bag on the floor beside Timmy's bed for me. She pulled up the blankets around Simon and sighed. "It's nice to see this room used again."

Sleep came slowly. Timmy's things were all around me—baseball glove on the side table, books on a shelf, fishing rod in the corner. Compared to Simon's room, Timmy's was neat—everything in its place. It reminded me of Gramps' room, his things as he'd left them, nothing moved or touched.

I slipped into a dream, the same dream as the night before, with Gramps in the forest. A shorter, slimmer man in the shadows. Dozens of other men carrying axes following them. Me, far behind.

We enter a clearing and in the distance I see a lake, its surface like liquid diamonds in the moonlight. Gramps turns, smiles, and waves to me. The man at his side turns too. For the first time, I see Tom Hendricks' features clearly.

Tom Hendricks waves, a hurry-up, come-and-join us type of wave. I wave back and run to catch up. The crowd parts to let me through, and soon I stand on the shore between the two men. My great-grandfather carries something—a small metal box. He smiles again, touches my shoulder, and passes the box to me.

I woke up then. Clatter from the kitchen and the smell of coffee drifted into the room. It had been just a dream. A simple dream. That's all.

But as I sat up, Timmy's things around me, the memory of the dream fresh in my head, I felt strangely satisfied. As if Gramps and Tom Hendricks had invited me to tell their story. As if they'd granted me permission to carry out my plan.

I shook Simon awake. "Whaa…where am I?" he said. He glanced at the clock and tossed back the sheets. "I forgot to call Dad. I am so dead."

"Relax. I called him last night."

While Simon got his bearings, I supplied a few details. Then I hit the bathroom, splashed cold water on my face, and smoothed down my stick-up hair.

"Hurry up, Simon," I called as I raced down the stairs.

Midway through my plate of toast and eggs, Simon rounded the corner, hair straight out like helicopter blades. He held an odd-looking contraption made of sticks, nails and a thick rubber band. "What is this?"

Marnie's mother smiled. "That was Timmy's. I'm not sure what it is."

"I bet it's a catapult. Maybe a slingshot." Simon wiggled onto a chair and placed the device on the table. "It's a weapon for sure."

"Timmy was always building things like that," she said.

"Cool!" Simon twisted a knob on the unusual device. "Wonder what this does?"

Mrs. Dohanski set a glass of orange juice on the table in front of him. She gazed at Simon then smoothed down his propeller blade hair. "Would you like to keep it, Simon?"

"Really? You serious?" He turned to me, eyes wide, a crescent-moon smile on his face. "Just think of the fun we'll have with this, Nate!'"

Between mouthfuls, I shared my dream and what I wanted to do. They agreed to help. Marnie made an important phone call. Simon powered up his cell phone. I sorted through the objects in my backpack.

Dad's silver car pulled up at noon. Buster bolted out as soon as the door opened. He danced around my legs and licked Simon's face, smothering him with slobbers. Olivia was right behind, dragging Barbie by the hair and Joe by the foot. I wrapped my arms around her.

"The envelope," she whispered in my ear. "I gave it to Gram like you asked."

I winked and ruffled her hair. "You did just fine, Ollie."

"The tree house. You promised, remember?"

"'Course I do. Soon as we get home."

Gram came next, looking haggard. She hugged me, long and hard. "I'm so glad you're both safe. I don't know what I would have done if—"

"I'm sorry," I said. "I should never have taken off like I did."

Mom hugged me too, but gasped when she saw the bandage on my head.

"I'm okay," I said. "Really, I'm fine."

Dad kept his distance. "This had better be good." He shot me a stern look. All things considered, his reaction was pretty tame. No angry outburst and no I-am-so-disappointed-in-you speech this time.

Minutes later, Mr. Sloan arrived in his red SUV. He hugged Simon, then looked him up and down. "I'm glad you're alright, kid, but you have a load of explaining to do."

"Did you bring—?" I asked Mr. Sloan.

"Of course." He winked and pointed to his car.

We travelled down the old road in two vehicles, churning dust as we bounced over ruts.

Other cars were parked at the trailhead, and the moment we pulled up, a short lady with a camera ran to greet us.

"You the one who called?" she asked Marnie.

Marnie smiled, spoke to the lady, and called Simon and me over. We beamed as the reporter from the Paradise Times snapped our picture.

"I don't get it," my father muttered. "What's this all about?"

"You'll see," I said.

We followed Buster as he raced down the path past the overturned logs to the largest of the concrete piles. Fortier was already there, carrying a cardboard box under one arm.

"Why Albert," Gram looked from him to me, clearly baffled. "What are you doing here? I thought you had gone fishing."

Fortier pointed in my direction. "This is Nate's idea."

Gram sat on the concrete pile while the others gathered around—my parents, Olivia, Mr. Sloan, Marnie's parents, the reporter with the camera.

"I still don't get it," Dad said.

Mr. Sloan shook his head. "Me neither."

"Just wait. You'll see," I said.

Fortier gave a short introduction. He talked about Northern Airways, the downed plane, and the missing shipment. He explained his role as an investigator for the Bank of Montreal.

"A fortune in gold coins, gone without a trace. I've spent twenty years searching for Shipment #35."

Gram looked to me, surprised. "Nate? I still don't understand."

"You will, Gram."

The reporter scribbled a few notes and snapped a picture of Fortier, a lopsided smile across his long face.

Fortier added a few more details. "There's a reward for the recovery of the gold. I believe we know where it is now. Once we locate the shipment, the reward will go to these three youngsters."

"What?" Dad said.

Mr. Sloan simply shook his head.

"Not only that," Mrs. Dohanski added. "These three might just have saved this whole area."

It was Marnie's turn. She talked about the hydro-electric dam, the threat of flooding, and the loss it would bring to the community of Paradise. "But now we have a chance of stopping it," she said.

The reporter scribbled on her notepad and took another picture.

"Now," I told Simon.

"My turn? Oh, good."

Simon pulled out his cell phone. Everyone huddled around as he flipped through his selfies and told the story of our adventure. "Here we are in my room. Here's—"

Olivia squinted and moved closer. "What's that?"

"Uh…." Simon hugged the phone to his chest—but not before I caught a peek of two buttheads and two butts in living colour.

A wave of heat flashed across my face.

Simon grinned and thumbed onto the next frame. With picture after picture he told the story—our bus trip to Paradise, the long walk to Whitewater Camp, our discoveries there. He dumped his oversized backpack on the ground, and held up each item. When he demonstrated his homemade metal detector, the group cheered.

"That's my boy," Mr. Sloan said, leaping up to slap Simon on the back.

But Simon had more to say. He talked about the bear, exaggerating a few details to add excitement. Then he showed the shelter where we'd taken refuge from the bear and spent our first night.

"You slept there?" Mom gasped.

Mr. Sloan shook his head. "Saved by peanut butter sandwiches. Unbelievable." Then he smiled and punched Simon in the arm. "That's my boy."

The reporter wrote a few notes and took a picture of a grinning Simon wearing his supply belt and holding the metal detector.

Now it was my turn. "Gram," I said. "I have something to show you."

We could see the lake from there, glassy smooth, the blue sky reflected in the still waters. I opened the *Garden Supplies* box I had carried down the trail, the one Mr. Sloan brought in his car. I took out the briefcase, shirt and other objects, and laid them on the ground. From Fortier's box, I retrieved the other things. Finally, I opened my backpack and took out Gramps' sketches, the small black book, the letter from the bank, and the crumpled photocopied pages. Last of all, I placed the metal box on the ground.

Then I told the story. I told Gram about Gramps, of his quest to find the truth as his mind was unraveling, of his travels to Paradise and the things he'd found there. I read passages from the flight log, and together we traced Tom Hendricks' journey from crash site, to lake's edge, to the powerhouse, to the place where his journey ended and ours was just beginning.

Finally, I took out the gold coin and sheet of paper from the metal box, and read the last paragraph written by Tom Hendricks.

> *To my loving family, I think of you often. In dreams I feel as though you are right beside me, keeping me warm. I don't know what the future holds, where fate will take me or if I will survive, but this I do know. You are all more precious to me than life itself. God-willing, one day we will be together again.*

Gram wiped away tears. "All this time, I thought he'd abandoned us... but he didn't. He was thinking of us in his last moments."

I passed her the fragile paper. She took it in wrinkled fingers and read it herself, her hand over her mouth. Fresh tears streamed down her cheeks.

Mom rushed up to give me a hug, while Dad slapped me on the back. "Now that's *my* boy," he said to Mr. Sloan.

The reporter gathered everyone together for one more picture. My parents and Olivia beside me. Mr. Sloan beside Simon. Marnie's parents beside her. Gram in the middle. Even Buster showed up, curling around my legs, right where he belonged.

As the reporter snapped the picture, a cool breeze fanned the forest. I couldn't help but think it was Gramps, stopping by for one last visit.

NOTES FROM THE AUTHOR

This is a fictional story, but many elements are based on fact:

Whitewater Prisoner of War Camp

The Whitewater prisoner of war camp as described in the story actually existed. In 1942, with the threat of a German invasion of Britain a strong possibility, the British government asked the Canadian government under the leadership of Prime Minister McKenzie King to accept several thousand German soldiers who had been captured in North Africa. Canada approved the request and established forty camps across the country to hold captured Germans. The Whitewater Lake camp in Manitoba's Riding Mountain National Park was one of these.

The arrangement benefited both Britain and Canada. With many Canadians serving in the armed forces, there was a shortage of able-bodied workers in Canada. Among other duties, the German prisoners at the Whitewater camp worked in the forests of Riding Mountain Park cutting badly-needed firewood to supply heat for Canadian homes throughout the winter. The prisoners were paid fifty cents for each half cord of wood they harvested.

The Whitewater location was considered ideal for a prisoner of war camp. Not only was it situated near thick stands of trees, but it was also remote and isolated enough to ensure that the German prisoners had little contact with Canadians living in villages and towns nearby. The prisoners selected for the Whitewater camp were considered low-risk for escape, and the camp was thought to be so secure that fences and enclosures were deemed unnecessary and so none were built.

The camp consisted of a number of buildings: six bunkhouses; a large cookhouse and dining room; quarters for staff; a hospital, barn, and even a powerhouse for generating electricity. Four hundred fifty prisoners were housed at the camp. To easily identify them, they were assigned a type of uniform—a pair of blue denim trousers with a red strip running down the outer legs and a shirt with a large red circle on the back.

Although the German prisoners worked hard, there was time for leisure activities too. Some of the men took up woodcarving. Others played in bands or acted in skits they wrote themselves. Several prisoners carved dug-out canoes from large spruce trees along the lakeshore and used the canoes to paddle to an island on the lake where they sometimes had bonfires.

Since the camp was fairly remote, security was loose. Some prisoners took advantage of this, sometimes escaping for jaunts into the forest or slipping away undetected on Saturday nights after roll-call to go to dances and parties in nearby towns, being sure to slip back into camp before roll-call again on Sunday morning.

Prisoners sometimes encountered bears while they worked in the forest. During a hike one spring day, forty prisoners came across a female and her two cubs. One of the cubs was captured and kept by the men as a camp mascot. During the winter, the bear hibernated under one of the buildings.

When the war ended, the camp was quickly dismantled. The work was started in the fall of 1945, but was interrupted by the early arrival of winter. It wasn't completed until the spring of 1946. All salvageable material was shipped to Dauphin, a town to the north of Riding Mountain National Park, to be held there for future auction. The buildings were purchased by a Winnipeg wrecking firm.

Today, little of the Whitewater camp survives. All that remains are a few concrete footings, the occasional circle of stones marking an old roadway, and, buried deep in the grass, the decaying shell of a long-abandoned dug-out canoe. In 2011, an archeological dig of the camp was started. Long buried artifacts are slowly being brought to the surface, each telling us more about an almost forgotten piece of Canadian history.

Paradise, Manitoba

The town of Paradise, Manitoba, described in this story is fictional. While there are hydro-electric construction projects in Manitoba, the one Paradise faces is also fictional. There are many small towns on the prairies that are similar to Paradise, and several that are a short drive from the Whitewater Camp. The town of Wassagaming in the heart of Riding Mountain National Park is the closest of these. Wassagaming is a tourist town, busy with visitors who come to enjoy recreational activities in nearby lakes and forests.

In Wassagaming, along a road that eventually connects to others leading to the Whitewater Camp, lies Pinewood Museum. A converted cottage, the small museum holds an array of memorabilia from around the area, and tucked into a corner, a display of photos from Whitewater Camp.

The Fort Dauphin Museum in Dauphin, Manitoba also contains information about the prisoner of war camp. Among its displays are two well-preserved dug-out canoes that were carved by German prisoners from spruce trees near Whitewater Lake.

Shipment #35

Neither Shipment #35 nor Northern Airways actually existed, but the story of the downed plane and its airmen is based loosely on a real incident. On December 11, 1931, a pilot and mechanic who were flying a bush plane to a northern community in Manitoba ran into a snowstorm and were forced to land on remote Charron Lake, three hundred ten kilometres northeast of Winnipeg. The men were found alive by rescuers two weeks later, but the plane, a rare Fokker Standard, became frozen in the ice. The following spring, the ice thawed and the plane sank in nearly forty metres of water. The location of the aircraft became lost. It wasn't until 2005, seventy-three years after the sinking, that a five-member search team discovered the submerged wreckage with the assistance of sophisticated sonar and bal-positioning equipment.

ACKNOWLEDGEMENTS

Many people contributed to this book in ways large and small. From its inception, I've been fortunate to have unwavering encouragement from family, friends, and fellow writers. To each I owe a debt of gratitude.

To Writer's Group (Lisa, Faith, Judy and Janet) who read the earliest and roughest draft, thanks for believing it was worth something.

To Vast Imaginations (Suzanne, Christina, Mindi and MaryLou) who read it later, thanks for coaching me to do better.

To the entire Rebelight team, for embracing the story and for amazing support throughout the process—thank you a thousand times over. To Deborah Froese, my primary editor, a bouquet of special thanks for helping me to fill gaps, add texture, and for teaching me so much about writing along the way.

To friends and family, your enthusiasm and interest mattered, always. Thank you.

To my home team—Ashley, Nick, Stephen, Kristy and little Rae—thank you for being there every minute to back me up and cheer me on.

Finally, to my wife, Jo, who's always been there, giving me full rein to write, fueling me with ideas, and telling "you can do it" whenever I doubted myself. Where would I be without you? Thanks, Jo.

CPSIA information can be obtained at www.ICGtesting.com
Printed in the USA
LVOW12s2046270515

440145LV00014B/150/P